"Maybe you should let them find you," she murmured, her gaze dipping to his mouth. Her own lips trembled apart, her breath quickening.

Answering heat flooded his body. "I told you. If you go, I'll follow."

"You're crazy." Somehow, she was even closer to him, her breasts brushing against his chest. He didn't know if she'd stepped closer or if he had been the one to close the distance.

He didn't really care.

"I rode bulls for a living," he answered, sliding one hand around to press against her spine, tugging her closer. "Crazy's baked into that cake, sweetheart."

She slipped her hands under the hem of his T-shirt, her fingers cool against his skin. She traced his muscles and the ridges of his rib cage with a light, maddening touch. "I don't need you."

"I think maybe you do."

DECEPTION LAKE

—

PAULA GRAVES

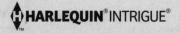

With thanks to Bill Clifton, the computer guru who answered all my questions with patience and kindness. All errors in this book are mine, not his.

Recycling programs for this product may not exist in your area.

ISBN-13: 978-0-373-74874-7

Deception Lake

Copyright © 2015 by Paula Graves

Printed in U.S.A.

www.Harlequin.com

Paula Graves, an Alabama native, wrote her first book at the age of six. A voracious reader, Paula loves books that pair tantalizing mystery with compelling romance. When she's not reading or writing, she works as a creative director for a Birmingham advertising agency and spends time with her family and friends. Paula invites readers to visit her website, paulagraves.com.

Books by Paula Graves

HARLEQUIN INTRIGUE

The Gates

Dead Man's Curve

Crybaby Falls

Boneyard Ridge

Deception Lake

Bitterwood PD

Murder in the Smokies

The Smoky Mountain Mist

Smoky Ridge Curse

Blood on Copperhead Trail

The Secret of Cherokee Cove

The Legend of Smuggler's Cave

Visit the Author Profile page at Harlequin.com for more titles

CAST OF CHARACTERS

Mara Jennings—Working at The Gates as an administrative assistant is just a cover for her real assignment: using her own computer skills to find an elusive hacker who may hold the key to a terror plot. But someone knows her secrets—and is willing to kill her to stop her.

Jack Drummond—The retired rodeo cowboy's past is littered with regrets—and breaking Mara's heart is his biggest regret of all. Now she's in danger, and protecting her may be his best chance of paying for his sins.

Mallory Jennings—Mara's twin sister was murdered four years ago. Could her unsolved murder be connected to the threats against Mara?

Alexander Quinn—The former CIA agent has kept Mara's real assignment secret, even in his own agency. But can he protect her when she goes rogue?

Riley and Hannah Patterson—Jack's brother-in-law and his wife are the only family Jack has left, and when he's in trouble, they're ready to help.

Endrex—The mysterious computer hacker seems to be right in the middle of a terror plot. But is he a good guy trying to stop the crime? Or has he gone to the dark side?

Carlos Herrera—Mallory Jennings's former lover turned out to be a very bad guy. Could he have been behind her murder—and the current threat to her twin?

Nick Darcy—One of two agents at The Gates who knows Mara's secrets. Could he have leaked the information to the people now targeting her?

Anson Daughtry—The computer guru at The Gates, fun-loving and laid-back, seems unlikely to be the leak at the agency. But are appearances deceiving?

Chapter One

The weather was warm for March in the Smokies, or so the woman at the diner counter informed Jack Drummond when he commented on the heat as he took a seat at the counter and scanned the large menu board behind her. She was a broad-shouldered woman in her late thirties, with work-worn hands and a plain but pleasant face devoid of makeup. The name tag over her left breast read *Darlene*.

"Won't last," Darlene warned in a hard-edged drawl as she pulled a pen and order pad from her apron pocket. "We'll get another frost in time to kill off all the daffodils that'll be blooming." She shrugged. "Spring in Tennessee."

Jack could tell Darlene a few stories about spring in Wyoming that would curl her lanky brown hair. Late-season snowstorms piling up in feet, not inches. Winds so strong and cold they seemed to blast the skin right off your face. But he refrained, ordering a steak sandwich and a sweet tea, his gaze sliding past the beer menu without snagging for even a second.

Progress.

The bell on the door behind him tinkled as another customer came in from the March sunshine. A woman's voice called out, husky and lightly tinted with a Texas twang. "Darlene, do you have the to-go orders for The Gates ready?"

The skin on Jack's neck prickled, and he swung his head slowly toward the newcomer, certain he'd imagined the familiar tones he'd heard in the feminine voice. She'd be too old or too young, too tall, too short, hair too red or not red enough, wrong eyes, wrong face, wrong build.

But not this time. In the middle of Purgatory, Tennessee, on an impromptu fishing trip with his brother-in-law's family, he'd finally tracked down Mara Jennings.

He'd been looking for her for four years to make amends.

It was one of the twelve steps, one he hadn't taken where Mara Jennings was concerned. But now that she was standing right in front of him, so close that he could lean forward a few inches and touch her arm, his tongue felt like lead and his pulse began to roar in his ears.

She must have felt his scrutiny, for her cool blue eyes flicked his way, her own gaze resting a brief moment on his face before sliding back to the waitress at the counter.

She hadn't recognized him.

Was that possible? He'd been a little lax about getting his hair cut since he left the rodeo circuit, and he'd put on ten pounds now that he wasn't shooting through gates on the back of a thousand pounds of pissed-off beef and trying to hang on for eight seconds of sheer adrenaline. But it wasn't his face that had gotten crushed under Coronado's rolling body. His looks hadn't changed that much.

Then her gaze snapped back, her brow creasing slightly as her eyebrows dipped to a V over her nose.

He managed to find his voice. "Hi, Mara."

She froze in place for a moment, her expression going completely blank. Then she gave a short nod. "Hi."

"So, this is where you disappeared to. I wondered." He licked his dry lips. "I was so sorry to hear about your sister."

A flicker of pain darted across her still face, so brief that he wondered if he'd imagined it. But when she spoke, her voice came out on a soft rasp. "Thank you."

"I'm sorry about everything, really. Especially the way things ended."

Her eyes narrowed slightly. "Forget about it, Jack. I have."

The hardness in her tone shouldn't have come as a surprise, given how badly he'd messed up the last time they saw each other. And the cool indifference should have been a relief, a reassurance that his selfish stupidity hadn't crushed her spirit completely.

But he couldn't shake the feeling that something was very, very wrong with Mara Jennings.

"I know it's been a long time, but I'd really like to talk to you a little more, try to explain a few things. Could you make some time for me?"

She shook her head. "Jack, I've moved on."

"There's still the matter of the money."

Her brow furrowed again, her eyes darting toward him before sliding away. "This is about money? Really?" She sounded confused.

Now he knew something was wrong.

"Seven thousand dollars, Mara. Plus four years of interest?"

Her lips pressed to a thin line. "Was there anything in writing?"

He stared at her, unease twisting a knot in his gut. "No, of course not. You know there wasn't." He took a step closer to her, unable to stop himself. "Are you okay?"

Alarm flickered in her eyes before she turned toward the waitress, who'd just returned to the counter with a box filled with individual brown paper sacks. She didn't answer his question as she pulled out a credit card and handed it to the waitress to process.

While Darlene was running the credit card through the system, Mara continued to ignore him, her small, round chin lifted with a hint of haughtiness he'd never seen in Mara Jennings during the year he'd known her.

He might not have changed much in four years, but clearly she had.

She took the credit card back from Darlene, signed the slip and picked up the box of lunch bags, then turned toward the door without even glancing his way. She was going to leave without saying anything else, he realized.

Part of him argued to just let her go. If she didn't want to deal with the past, he shouldn't make her.

But there was still the issue of the money.

Before he could keep his feet from moving, he'd stepped into her path, forcing her to stop so quickly she almost dropped the box of lunches she carried. He caught the sliding box and steadied it for her, his fingers brushing over hers.

Her gaze snapped up to meet his, and she took a quick step backward. "What do you want?"

"I get that you don't want to deal with the past. I'm not asking you to forgive me or anything like that. But seven thousand dollars is a lot of money—"

"And you just said there was nothing in writing." Her husky voice was edged with disdain. "So you can't prove I owe you a damn thing. Now excuse me."

She passed him quickly and left through the front door of the diner, passing Jack's brother-in-law, Riley Patterson, and his wife and child as they entered. Riley's craggy face split with a grin at the sight of Jack standing in the middle of the diner. "What did you do, strike out with the redhead?"

Riley's wife, Hannah, lowered her son, Cody, to the floor so he could hurry over to Jack. Reaching down, he picked up the three-year-old, tucked him close and looked over his head at Riley. "Do you remember me telling you about needing to make amends to a woman I hurt in Amarillo?"

Riley's smile faded. "Was that her?"

"I thought it was," Jack answered, remembering the cold, haughty air of the woman he'd just watched leave the diner. "I guess it is." He waved toward an empty booth, inviting them to take a seat. He settled onto the bench seat across from them, setting Cody down beside him. "But something very strange is going on."

"Strange how?" Hannah asked before Riley could speak.

"Well, I brought up the seven thousand dollars, and she acted like she didn't remember it at all. Which was weird enough. But when I pressed her on it—" He shook his head, the flutter of unease in his gut returning. "She asked me if we put anything in writing, and when I told her of course not, she said I couldn't prove she owed me a thing."

Hannah and Riley exchanged a quick look. "Are you sure you didn't misunderstand?" Riley asked.

"Believe me, I didn't." He shook his head. "Four years after the fact, she doesn't remember that I scammed seven thousand dollars from her. How is that even possible?"

Don't panic. There's *no need to panic.*

She entered through the front door of the two-story Victorian mansion on Magnolia Street, breathing deeply through her nose and releasing both air and tension through her mouth with each determined step. The office conference room was about ten paces down the narrow central corridor, and she timed her respiration accordingly—one breath, three steps. By the time she knocked on the door and received the invitation to enter, she had managed to present an outward air of calm.

But inside, she was freaking out completely.

Of all people to run into here in Purgatory, Tennessee—Jack Drummond? The cowboy with a heart of stone.

God, she'd been loathing that name for four years, loathing even the mere thought of what he'd done, the wreckage he'd left behind. She'd even wished him a painful end underneath some bucking bronc or twisting bull more than once, but she'd never figured she'd actually find out what happened to him after he left the dust of Amarillo behind him.

Well, now she knew. He was alive, well and disgustingly handsome.

But what the hell was he doing in Tennessee?

She entered the conference room quietly and set the box on the long credenza that took up most of the length of the nearest wall. Someone had already started a pot of coffee brewing, and she slipped back out of the conference room to retrieve a cooler of ice cubes for the two dozen bottles of water, juice and soft drinks lined up like soldiers at attention on one end of the sideboard.

Halfway there, she heard footsteps behind her and shot a quick look down the hall. The Gates'

CEO, Alexander Quinn, was coming up the hall behind her, his expression impossible to read. As usual.

She turned to face him. "Did I forget something?"

"What happened while you were out?"

She thought about trying to lie, but Quinn had spent a couple of decades in the CIA. Seeing through lies was part of his business. "I ran into someone from the past. From Texas."

Quinn's eyes narrowed. "I see."

"He wanted me to fork over seven thousand dollars. I didn't know what he was talking about, so I sort of faked it, but—"

"But you're not sure he believed you?"

"No."

Quinn was silent for a moment, his hazel eyes holding her gaze without making her feel uncomfortable. For a man who had lived on lies and adrenaline, he had a calming effect on most people, and she wasn't immune herself. "What's his name?"

"Jack Drummond."

"Can you give me a description?"

"Black hair, worn kind of longish. Brown eyes. Olive-toned skin. I believe he's part Shoshone—he's from up in Wyoming originally.

He's not super tall—maybe six feet, six-one. Big shoulders, narrow waist and hips. Cowboy."

Quinn arched one eyebrow.

"No, literally a cowboy. He was on the rodeo circuit back in Texas and the Southwest."

"What's he doing in Tennessee?"

"I didn't ask, and he didn't say."

Quinn looked at her a moment longer with that calm, thoughtful expression that made her feel as if he were trying to hypnotize her. Then he gave a short nod. "Go ahead and get the ice. Don't worry about Jack Drummond. He won't be a problem."

She knew Quinn had the means to protect her from her past. And because he needed the skills she offered when she wasn't playing office gofer, she knew he'd be diligent about it.

But Quinn couldn't erase the memory of Jack Drummond's dark eyes or sexy voice from her brain as she grabbed the clean cooler from the storage closet and started scooping ice into it.

She might hate Jack Drummond's guts and never want to see him again. But she doubted very seriously she could ever stop worrying about him, now that he'd invaded her world again. Had meeting him here in Purgatory been nothing but a strange coincidence?

Or was something a lot more sinister at work?

"THE GATES?" HANNAH looked up from wiping Cody's lunch off his hands and face at Jack's question. "I wonder if she was talking about Alexander Quinn's private investigation agency. It's right here in Purgatory."

Riley returned from grabbing more napkins from the counter and handed them to Hannah. "What about Alexander Quinn?"

"That private-eye agency he runs now—isn't it called The Gates?"

"Yeah, it is. Sutton Calhoun works there now."

"Right." Hannah made another swipe at the mess Cody had made with his peanut-butter-and-jelly sandwich. "He used to work at Cooper Security, but I think he was from up this way to begin with."

Jack tamped down his impatience and kept his tone even. "So The Gates is a detective agency?"

"Yeah. Well, investigations and security, I guess. Maybe your friend Mara works there. You could probably ask that waitress and she could tell you where to find the place." Riley's gaze sharpened. "If that's really what you want to do."

"I need to give her the money. It's sitting in my bank, taunting me."

Hannah's lips twitched at his description, and he didn't really blame her for finding his description a bit melodramatic. When his sister-in-law had met him, not long after he'd left Amarillo, he was sober only a couple of months, and the call of the rodeo still roiled in his blood. She'd been in Wyoming on vacation, ended up in the middle of a serial murder investigation and had come close to losing her life.

But Riley had been there, watching her back. Keeping her safe.

Falling in love, after grieving for three long, lonely years.

Jack's sister Emily had been Riley's first love. His first wife. Her murder had come damn close to destroying both Riley and Jack, though in different ways.

Riley's response had been to close himself off to all but a few close friends. And to Jack. But Riley's growing obsession with solving Emily's murder had eaten away at Jack's soul. Solving the murder wasn't going to bring Emily back. And Emily had been all that was left of Jack's dysfunctional family.

So he'd gone to Texas, moved his base of operations to a little town just west of Amarillo. He'd buried himself in boots and spurs and rodeo groupies who longed to ride a cowboy a whole lot longer than eight seconds.

Then he'd met Mara Jennings, who was anything but a groupie. Fool that he was, he'd considered her a challenge he couldn't resist, when he should have run as far and as fast from a woman like her as he could.

The groupies knew the score. They weren't interested in forever with a cowboy. They just wanted the excitement for a few days out of the year when the rodeo came to town.

Mara Jennings had "forever" written in her pretty blue eyes and winsome smile, and he should have known he'd break her heart.

Hell, maybe he *had* known it.

He just hadn't cared at that point in his life.

"I've had some dealings with Quinn," Hannah said thoughtfully as she handed her slightly sticky son to Riley. "I could just casually drop by the agency to say hi, and if you just happened to be with me and your friend just happened to be there—"

"If you just happen to be matchmaking, Hannah, you can forget it. Mara Jennings is not the woman for me. She never was."

That had been the problem.

"Well, maybe you could tell Quinn about the money you owe her, then," Hannah said.

"I think I'll just fly under the radar, if you don't mind. But good idea about talking to the waitress." He slid from the booth and headed to the counter, where the waitress was wiping down the surface with a clean rag.

She looked up with a weary smile as Jack

stopped in front of her. "Can I get you something else?"

"Actually I could use some directions. I have an old friend who works here in Purgatory at a place called The Gates—ever heard of it?"

"Sure, everybody has. Your friend one of the investigators?"

"Right." He searched his brain for the name Riley had mentioned. "Sutton Calhoun."

"Oh, he's such a nice guy. Real good-lookin', too." Darlene's cheeks grew pink and she shot Jack a sheepish smile. "His wife's a cop over in Bitterwood. They come in now and then."

"I thought I'd surprise him at the office, since he doesn't know I'm in town. Can you point me in the right direction?"

"Well, you're on the right street, actually. Just take a right when you leave, go a couple of blocks in that direction and you'll see a big white Victorian mansion right at the corner of Magnolia Street and Laurel Avenue. There's a pair of large iron gates at the entrance. Can't miss it."

Riley and Hannah met him at the door. "What are you planning to do?" Riley asked.

"I don't know," Jack admitted. "Approaching her directly didn't do me a lot of good."

"I hate to mention this," Hannah said quietly, "but you're starting to sound a little stalkerish."

Jack slanted a look at her. "I'm not obsessed with Mara."

"But you're about to track her down at her office after she told you to get lost," Riley pointed out as he picked up Cody and settled his son on his hip. "She doesn't even seem to remember that you nicked seven grand from her. Maybe you should just let it go, too."

"And that doesn't strike you as strange? That she's forgotten losing seven grand? Mara wasn't rich. Seven thousand dollars was a lot to her."

"Maybe she considers it a small price to pay for getting you out of her life." Riley's tone of voice was gentle, but the truth behind his words was harsh. Jack couldn't quite keep from flinching.

"Why don't you come out fishing with us this afternoon instead?" Hannah suggested. Apparently she'd gotten over her matchmaking urge.

"You know, I think I'll just wander around town this afternoon. See the sights."

Riley glanced around the sleepy street in front of them, his eyebrows notching upward. "What sights?"

"Go fish," Jack said firmly, heading for his truck. "I'll catch up with you later at the motel." He didn't wait for them to answer, sliding into the cab of the truck and starting the engine.

The radio was tuned to a rock station out of

Knoxville; Led Zeppelin's "Kashmir" was about halfway through the guitar and drum riff. He turned it up and pulled out into the light traffic on Magnolia Street, heading right.

He spared a glance in the rearview mirror. Riley and Hannah stood by their own truck, Cody still on Riley's hip. Jack felt like a jerk for bailing on them, but the truth was, he didn't want to be talked out of approaching Mara Jennings one more time.

He owed her a hell of a lot more than the seven thousand dollars with interest he'd taken from her.

But money was all he had to offer.

SHE USUALLY WORKED until five, but around three Quinn told her to take the rest of the day off. He could probably tell she was too wired to be any good to anyone at the agency, and she could always use the extra time at her cabin to work on the side project Quinn had given her.

It was why she was working at The Gates in the first place.

The mild afternoon warmth had abated with the arrival of storm clouds brewing in the west, and a crisp chill edged the breeze blowing at her back as she crossed the road to where she'd parked her little blue Mazda car. At least the car's interior was still warm; she snuggled into the seat as she pulled away from the curb and headed east toward the mountains and the cabin she rented on Deception Lake.

She'd thought the seclusion would be just what she needed. No nosy neighbors, no loud music coming from apartments next door. Deception Lake's power grid seemed stable, and her connection to the internet was solid. It was really the prime situation for her side project, and until she'd run into Jack Drummond at the diner, she had felt relatively safe.

Funny how one unexpected encounter from the past could knock your whole world off its axis.

The cabin was on the eastern edge of the lake, butted up to Fowler Mountain, where bigger houses dotted the mountain face, vacation homes and rentals that probably brought in a pretty penny for the landowner. She was renting from Alexander Quinn himself, however, so he'd given her a break on the rent in return for her putting in some hours as an assistant at The Gates.

That was her cover story, she knew. Quinn didn't always like to share information even with people he had trusted enough to hire.

She parked her car on the gravel drive outside the cabin and cut the engine, sitting in the ensuing silence and just listening. Later in the summer, there would be families out on the water or inhabiting the cabins farther along the lakeshore, their happy cries and laughter drifting over the water to encroach on the quiet. But not yet. March was too cool for swimming, and most of the best spring fishing could be found in other parts of the lake, so boats rarely made it this far down the water.

Nobody knew she was here. She was as safe as she'd ever been.

So why, when she stepped out of the car and started toward the low front porch of the cabin, did she feel as if she were being watched?

Don't be stupid, she scolded herself with an upward tilt of her chin. *You're Mara Caroline Jennings, and you don't attract crazies the way your sister, Mallory, did.*

She reached the porch and put her hand out to open the door.

But it was already opening.

A man dressed in dark forest camouflage stepped out on the porch and pushed a large pillowcase down over her head, wrapping her up in a tight grasp that squeezed the air right out of her lungs.

As she gasped for breath, trying feebly to struggle against the iron grip, she realized with a rush of fear that she'd never get away from Mallory Jennings, no matter how far she ran.

Chapter Two

Jack kept several car lengths back as he followed Mara Jennings out of town onto a winding rural road leading eastward, toward the mountains. They were still mostly in the foothills here in Purgatory, and for a man who'd grown up with the Grand Teton Mountains practically in his backyard, the softly rounded peaks of the Smoky Mountains might have seemed a letdown if it weren't for the fact that the whole area was hilly and lush green, even in March before the spring growth had had a chance to bud completely.

Up in the higher elevations, evergreens like spruce, firs and pines maintained their verdant splendor all winter, lending the mountains a soft blue-green hue filtered by the ever-present haze of mist. Even down here in the lower elevations, the hardwoods were starting to sprout the first leaves of spring, and within a few short weeks, the place would be alive again after the long winter.

But there wasn't enough greenery to hide him from the woman in the Mazda car a hundred yards ahead of him, so he stayed as far from her as he could until she turned off the highway and seemed to drive straight into the woods.

Slowing the truck as he neared the point where the Mazda car had disappeared, he saw there was a narrow two-lane road leading through the woods to points unknown. Probably the lake, he deduced, having caught a glimpse of sunlight sparkling off the water's surface just before the woods grew denser, blocking the view.

Even as he turned onto the two-lane road and followed it, he wondered if Hannah and Riley had been right to worry about him. What the hell did he think he was going to accomplish by following her from work? Was she going to be more receptive of his need for restitution if she thought he was nuts?

He started looking for the first place he could turn the truck around and head back out of the woods, but as he drew close to what looked like a gravel driveway, he spotted the little blue Mazda car parked in front of a small cabin nestled in the center of a tiny clearing in the woods. The woods in front of the cabin thinned out until they reached the sandy shore of the lake about fifty yards from the cabin.

He pulled the truck to a stop at the edge of the

driveway and let the engine idle a moment as he considered his options. Then, out of the corner of his eye, he spotted movement on the cabin's front porch.

It took a second to process what he was seeing. A second more to let his sluggish brain catch up with the adrenaline rushing through his body like water pouring through a breach in a dam.

Then his cowboy instincts kicked in and he was out of the truck and running toward the violent struggle playing out on the cabin porch.

Jack wasn't currently armed, his Colt M1911 stashed in the locker in the bed of his truck. But the man struggling with Mara didn't appear to be armed, either.

And Jack didn't plan to give him time to go for a weapon if he was.

The sound of his boots crunching across the gravel didn't seem to have any effect on the wrestling match going on between Mara and her captor, but when Jack hit the first porch step, the man in camouflage froze for a moment.

That was when Mara struck, first with an elbow straight to the man's solar plexus, then followed up with a hard stomp on the man's instep and a simultaneous fist to the groin.

Slipping free of the man's suddenly floundering grasp, Mara flung herself away, giving Jack a clear shot. He hit the larger man at a full run, slamming him back into the cabin wall.

But a second later, the man in camo fought back, knocking Jack away with one brutal punch in the center of his chest. Jack fell backward, tumbling hard down the porch steps. His head hit the gravel with a jarring thud, and what air was left in his lungs after the man's first punch exploded from his chest on impact against the hard-packed soil.

For a second, Jack could see nothing but stars on a deep black field. But slowly, the sparkling darkness faded into waning daylight filtering through the thick canopy of trees surrounding the cabin.

And in the center of his vision, the barrel of a big, lethal-looking Smith & Wesson M&P40.

What small amount of air had managed to re-introduce itself to his lungs froze in place. He let his gaze move up the barrel to the small hand closed around the grip, then farther upward until he was staring into a pair of angry blue eyes.

"Are you with him?" Mara asked, her voice shaking but her hand steady.

"What?" he croaked, barely finding enough breath to answer.

"Are you with him?" she repeated, keeping the pistol trained on him as she nodded toward the woods. Her hair was a mess from the pillowcase the man had tried to use as a hood, and her eyes looked bloodshot and wild. He had a feeling she'd put a bullet into him first and ask questions later if he so much as blinked his eyes the wrong way.

"No. You didn't see me trying to stop him?"

Her lips pressed to a thin line. "Maybe you're trying to trick me."

"I'm not trying to trick you."

She didn't look appeased. "Get up."

He eased himself to a sitting position, wincing at the ache in his head. He felt something warm slithering down his scalp. "I think I'm bleeding."

She didn't look interested in his self-diagnosis. "Why did you come here? Are you stalking me?"

"No." At her look of skepticism, he added, "Not intentionally."

"Why did you approach me at the diner?"

He grimaced as she leaned toward him, bringing the barrel of the M&P40 even closer to his face. "Could you please put that thing away before you shoot me?"

"Not a chance," she answered in a flat tone. "Get up. All the way up."

He eased to his feet, aching tension knotting the muscles of his back and abdomen. "I'm definitely not with that guy. And I'm not a stalker, appearances to the contrary notwithstanding."

For a second the corner of her lips twitched.

But he chalked it up to a nervous tic, because the last thing he saw in those sharp, watchful blue eyes was anything approaching humor.

"You followed me here." It wasn't a question.

"I did," he admitted.

"Why?"

"To see where you were going." As an explanation, his answer was pathetic. That it was also true was of little importance.

"You've accomplished that," she said in a flat tone. "Now leave."

There was a curious note to her husky voice, a hint of vulnerability peeking through the tiny crack in her mask of contemptuous calm.

"Do you know who that guy was?"

She didn't answer, which he supposed was answer enough.

"What are you involved in, Mara?"

He waited for an angry glare. But it never came.

"You need to leave. Now," she said, her tone unyielding. But she lowered the pistol to her side.

"Are you in trouble? Is there someone out there just waiting for me to leave to take another crack at you?"

Her only answer was to turn toward the cabin door.

Despite the throbbing pain in his head, he

forced himself up the steps, reaching the door just before it snapped closed behind her. He stuck his boot into the narrowing breach, stopping the door from shutting.

She glared at him through the narrow opening, but at least she left the pistol down by her side. "I said leave."

"I heard you."

"And yet you're still here."

Guilt fluttered in the center of his chest as her expression grew hard and cold. Mara Jennings had never been hard or cold, even when she should have been. Her kind, forgiving nature had made her an easy mark for his pathetic neediness, and he'd come to depend on her being there, being willing to overlook his copious flaws, whenever he needed her.

He supposed it was good she'd finally drawn a line he couldn't cross. He just hated that he'd been the one to add that hardness and coldness to her sweet nature.

"There's still the matter of seven thousand dollars," he said.

Taking a step back, she let go of the door. Pressed by his boot, it swung open, and he took a step inside, his gaze taking in the small front room. What he saw nearly stole his breath again.

The place had been completely wrecked.

THE TROUBLED LOOK on Jack Drummond's face was the only warning she got. Following his dark gaze, she saw what she'd missed in her earlier agitation.

Whatever else the intruder might have wanted, he'd made a shambles of her cabin. Ripped-up sofa cushions lay scattered about the room, fluffy clumps of foam and fiberfill stuffing littering the floor. Books had been pulled from the built-in shelves and discarded. A floor lamp lay on its side, the glass shade shattered.

Every ounce of adrenaline seemed to drain from her body in a flood, leaving her boneless and despairing.

"Who did this?" Jack's deep voice rumbled up her spine.

"Who do you think?"

"But why?"

She turned to meet his troubled gaze. "I have no idea."

Which was a lie, of course. She had a couple of pretty good ideas, actually. She just wasn't sure which one was the right one.

"Should we call the police?"

Her nerves reawakened in a rattling jangle. "No."

"Your boss?"

She thought about it briefly. Quinn would know what to do. But could she really trust him?

She knew the man's interest in her was anything but altruistic. He might be her boss, he might even have been her savior at a particularly dangerous time of her life, but he wasn't her friend.

She didn't have any friends. Not anymore.

"You need to go," she said in lieu of an answer.

"And what if that guy comes back?"

"He won't," she said, even though she knew someone would come back eventually. The only thing of value in this cabin was her computer system, and it was locked behind about five levels of physical security. And even if someone had stolen the computers themselves, they'd have had one hell of a time trying to get past her digital security.

She might look like an ordinary woman these days, but she wasn't.

She wasn't ordinary at all.

"Okay, if that's what you want, I'll go." Jack's voice was outwardly calm, but she heard a thread of discord vibrating just beneath the surface. "But I need just one more question answered."

She sighed. "What's that?"

"Why on earth do you think you owe me seven thousand dollars when you know as well as I do that I stole that money from you?"

Her stomach knotted painfully. Well, hell.

"Has something happened to you, Mara?

You didn't remember me right away today at the diner. You didn't remember anything about the money. And right now you're looking at me as if you've never seen me before." He took a step closer to her, his movement slow and careful, as if he expected her to bolt.

He wasn't entirely wrong. Even now she could feel the muscles bunching in her legs, as if her body was instinctively preparing for flight.

"A lot has happened," she answered in a carefully neutral tone. "I lost my sister. I left everything I knew to make a new start. And I didn't expect to see you here in Tennessee."

"That's not an answer."

"It's all you're going to get."

"Okay." He reached inside his jacket.

Adrenaline stormed her system again, and she brought up the pistol to bear on him. "Don't."

He stared at her, his dark eyes wide. "My God, Mara. What's happened to you?"

"Take your hand out of your jacket." To her dismay, her voice trembled. But her hand, at least, remained steady.

"I have a cashier's check for the seven thousand plus interest. That's all I was reaching for."

"I don't need the money. I don't want it."

"I need to give it to you." His voice sharpened. "I owe it to you, Mara, and if I don't do this—"

"Give it to a charity."

His eyes narrowed. "Your place just got trashed and you're telling me you couldn't use seven thousand dollars to fix the damage and buy you a new sofa?"

Of course she could use it. She just couldn't take it. Not from him. Not this way.

"Just give it to a charity. Wounded Warrior Project or Goodwill or St. Jude's—anything you want. If you want your sins off your conscience, do it that way. I'm not in the business of absolution."

His dark eyes snapped with a flare of anger, but it was gone almost as soon as it arose. "Fine." He removed his hand from his jacket and reached up to touch the back of his head, wincing as he did so. When he brought his hand in front of him, his fingers were sticky with blood.

For a second, she flashed back to that night, four years ago, when she'd come home to a house on fire and her sister lying dead on the living room floor. She'd known, in the brief seconds she'd had to make her decision, that there was nothing she could do anymore for her twin. The blood pooling around her sister's head painted a gruesome picture of what had happened while she was away picking up takeout for their dinner.

Her sister had been murdered, the fire set to cover up evidence.

And, for better or worse, she'd let it burn.

"I don't suppose you have a first-aid kit handy in all this mess?" he asked quietly, his gaze still focused on his bloody fingers.

The urge to push him and his bleeding head out of her cabin was nearly overwhelming. But he might be more injured than she thought, and the last thing she needed on her own conscience was another death.

"Find somewhere to sit down," she said, blowing out some of her frustration on a gusty sigh. "I'll see if my kit's still in one piece."

The rest of the cabin had been tossed as ruthlessly as the front room, but whatever the burly man in the camouflage had been looking for, he seemed to have left empty-handed. The first-aid kit was on the bathroom floor, its contents scattered over the gray tile. Most of the kit's components remained in sealed sterile packaging, however, so she scooped up the pieces and put them back inside the soft canvas kit, then took a minute to wash her hands before returning with the kit to the front room.

Jack had picked up an overturned ladder-back chair from the tiny dining area and sat at the table, wiping his bloody fingers on a paper towel salvaged from a roll that had been ripped from the wall-mounted holder. He looked up when she reentered the room. "I think there may be blood-stains on your rug in there," he said, nodding toward the area closer to the front door as he pressed the paper towel to the back of his head.

"How's your balance?" she asked, trying to remember the symptoms of a concussion. He'd never lost consciousness, that she could tell, and he didn't seem dizzy or wobbly on his feet—all good signs.

"Fine," he answered. "I don't have a concussion, if that's what you're worried about."

"You can't know that." She set the first-aid kit on the table next to him and unzipped the canvas bag.

"I rode bulls for a living for a decade," he said in a dust-dry tone. "I know the symptoms of a concussion better than I know my own name."

Mention of his occupation sent a dart of irritation shooting through her. "Rode?" she asked quietly.

"I've retired."

She slanted a quick look at him, taking in the lean angles and chisel-sharp planes of his ruggedly attractive face. "Your decision or the bull's?"

His lips quirked slightly, cutting deep dimples into both cheeks. "Definitely the bull's. He landed on me and broke my pelvis in several places. Doctors managed to knit me back together, but there are injuries even an insane cowboy like me can't gut his way back from."

His tone was neutral enough, but just as before, she sensed a darker emotion roiling under the surface.

"Bummer," she murmured, not meaning to sound as flippant as she did.

His gaze clashed with hers. "Yeah."

"I didn't mean—"

"Doesn't matter," he said quickly, looking away.

"Let me take a look at your head," she suggested, feeling both a flutter of guilt and answering anger for letting herself give enough of a damn about this confounding man to feel guilt in the first place.

Jack turned his head away from her so she could take a look at his injury. She bit back a gasp.

There was a split in the skin at least two inches long, the ragged edges of the wound raw and bloody. His thick, dark hair had absorbed a lot of the blood, but enough was still flowing to feed her alarm.

"Jack, you need stitches. And probably a CAT scan."

And she needed, more than anything, to get this man out of her house before he figured out the truth.

Chapter Three

"Do you have anyone I can call?" Mara's husky voice drew Jack's attention away from the medical forms he was busy filling out one-handed. His other hand was still pressing her bloody towel to the back of his head, where the jagged tear in his scalp continued spilling fresh blood. The clinic was busy, and a nurse had already come out to examine the wound and check his pupils before she deemed him in no great rush for treatment. A receptionist had then traded his insurance card and copay for a clipboard with three pages of medical forms to fill out.

He hadn't made it to the third page of the forms yet, but if the first two were anything to go by, he'd be spilling his sexual history, cataloging every freckle, mole or scar he possessed and outlining at least three generations of genealogy before he was done.

He looked away from the paperwork to answer Mara's question, relieved at a chance to stop writing. "My brother-in-law and his wife are with me here in town, but I don't want to worry them—"

"It's just—I have things to do."

He slanted his gaze toward her. "You're planning to leave here alone?"

Her brow furrowed. "Yes."

"Someone tried to kidnap you, Mara. Hell, we should have gone straight to the cops instead of coming here."

She frowned. "Keep your voice down."

He glanced around the full waiting room. Nobody was paying them any attention. "You're not planning to ignore this, are you?"

She looked away, not answering.

"Have you lost your mind?"

"No." Her voice remained soft and controlled. "You don't know anything about my life or my options. Don't pretend you do."

"What makes you think whoever attacked you this afternoon isn't waiting for you at your cabin right now?"

"I'm not your concern."

She was right. She wasn't his concern, or shouldn't have been. But the thought of letting her leave the clinic by herself was enough to make his chest tighten with alarm. "If you don't call the police, I will."

Her glare was lethal. "I'll tell them the intruder was you."

"What?" He stared back at her, certain he'd misunderstood.

"If you call the police," she said in a calm tone, "I'll tell them you were the intruder who trashed my place. That you're an ex-boyfriend who stalked me here all the way from Texas and wouldn't take no for an answer."

Anger built in his gut, hot and painful. "You'd lie about me to the police?"

Her gaze snapped toward him. "Only if you force me to."

"What the hell happened to you?" He lowered his voice, matching her tone. "I get that you probably hate me for the way I treated you, but you were never a liar."

"How would you know?" She looked down at her clasped hands. "You never really knew me at all, did you? You only ever saw what you wanted."

"I know you were kind." He watched her fingers twisting around each other, noticed the short, unpainted nails and wondered when she'd stopped getting manicures. It had been one of her few indulgences, her biweekly manicures. She'd been nearly obsessive about nail polish, eager to try all the newest colors and styles. "You were sweet and honest."

"Kind, sweet and honest gets you kicked in the teeth," she murmured.

"You mean, by drunk and stupid cowboys."

She angled her gaze up at him briefly but didn't answer.

"I guess I deserve that."

Her gaze dropped to the clipboard in his lap. "If you don't finish filling those out, the doctor will never get to you."

With a sigh, he turned his attention back to the papers and answered the rest of the questions. He half expected her to bolt the second he turned his back on her to bring the forms to the reception desk, but she was still sitting there in the corner of the waiting room when he returned.

"You said your brother-in-law and his wife. She's not your sister?"

"No. You know she's not." He stared at her, wondering how she could have forgotten the things he'd told her about Emily. She'd held his hand late into the night when he first shared the story of his sister's murder and how it had ripped away what was left of his family.

How could she even ask such a question?

"Mr. Drummond?" A pretty blonde nurse stuck her head through the door leading back to the examination area.

Jack turned to Mara. "Please stay until I'm

finished with the doctor. Let me ride home with you and make sure the cabin's secure."

She just gave a brief nod toward the waiting nurse. "Don't lose your place in line."

With one more backward glance at Mara to make sure she wasn't already making her escape, he followed the nurse back to the exam room.

HE THOUGHT SHE was going to bug out on him. She could tell by the wary look in his eyes as he glanced her way before following the nurse through the door.

He was right. She was.

She waited another minute to make sure he wasn't going to dart right back out to the waiting room to check on her, then grabbed her purse and headed out the clinic door. Her heart pounding frantically against her breastbone, she looked up and down the street, trying to figure out where to go next.

Rain clouds gathered in the west, swallowing the setting sun. A few fat raindrops splattered her car's windshield as she slid inside and sat for a second, willing her nerves to stop jangling.

She hadn't even had a chance to think about the man at the cabin, or what he'd wanted, thanks to Jack Drummond and his damn inconvenient head wound.

How had Jack found her cabin? Did he follow her from the office?

Why hadn't she noticed him following her?

She was losing her edge. Letting Alexander Quinn's calm competence and promises of protection lull her into a sense of security as false as everything else about her life. The woman she used to be would never have put her trust in an ex-spook with his own agenda.

She'd have trusted no one.

She had to go back to the cabin. She had to make sure the intruder hadn't had a chance to come back and breach the security of the safe room where all her work was hidden, and then, if everything was still there, she had to store it safely until she could get out of Purgatory and find her next bolt-hole.

She parked her car on a shallow turnaround just off the gravel road leading to her rental cabin, going the rest of the way on foot so she wouldn't announce her arrival, in case the intruder had come back. She kept her Smith & Wesson pistol in her shooting hand, her finger on the index point above the trigger the way Quinn had trained her to carry a loaded weapon. She supposed she owed him that much gratitude—over the course of the six years since she first met the man in a Colombian hellhole, he'd equipped her to handle the trouble she always managed to find.

Her cell phone vibrated in the front pocket of her jeans. After an initial jarring rattle of nerves, she ignored the hum and it finally subsided. Probably Quinn checking on her. She'd call him back so he didn't worry.

But not before she was packed and ready to get the hell out of Tennessee.

The cabin lay silent about thirty yards ahead of her, just visible through the thicket of trees. She went very still, watching and listening. The gathering storm was rolling in on a gusty northeastern wind, the mostly bare limbs of hardwood trees rattling like bones amid the whisper of evergreen boughs swishing back and forth.

But she heard nothing coming from the cabin. Pausing a moment longer, she tried to tap into the old instincts that had kept her alive so far. But she didn't feel any threat coming from the place she'd called home for the past five months.

She walked toward the cabin, scanning the woods around her for any unseen threat. She'd made it within fifteen yards of the cabin when a flash of sunlight on chrome snagged her gaze, and she stared with dismay at the big black Ford pickup truck tucked just off the road near her house.

Jack Drummond's truck. Of course. In her

stupid haste to hurry home and get packed up for her move, she'd forgotten all about Jack Drummond's damn pickup truck.

She looked away resolutely. Not her problem. He could get his brother-in-law to bring him to pick it up when he was through at the clinic. Surely she'd be out of here by then. At that point, it wouldn't matter what Jack Drummond thought.

She'd locked the front door to the cabin when she left earlier to take Jack into town to the clinic. It was still locked, and after a quick look around the cabin, she reassured herself that she was alone this time.

Shoving the pistol into the compact concealed-carry holster snapped to the waistband of her jeans, she stopped in the middle of the front room and surveyed the mess. Thanks to Jack's bleeding head wound, she hadn't even had a chance to pick up the ruined cushions or shattered lamp stand.

She wondered how he was doing, and the fact that she was sparing even a second of thought to the irritating man just pissed her off even more. Shoving her concerns aside, she crossed to the mahogany armoire that took up most of the back wall of the dining area and opened the door.

Inside, where most visitors might assume she kept her dinnerware and linens, was a second door, fitted with an electronic keypad. The perks of renting a cabin from a former spook, she thought with a grimace as she punched in the code and the door lock disengaged.

Beyond the steel-reinforced door lay a small room about the size of a walk-in pantry, which was apparently what it had been at one time. There had been shelves lining the walls when Quinn bought the place, he'd told her, but he'd removed them to make room for her computer equipment.

Equipment she was about to have to destroy, just as soon as she finished loading her files to the secure flash drives she'd purchased.

And the sooner she got to work, the sooner she could leave the dust of Purgatory, Tennessee, behind her.

"SHE DITCHED YOU at an urgent-care clinic without even waiting to see if you had a head injury?" Riley's eyebrows nearly reached his hairline as he walked with Jack out to the clinic's parking lot. "Good Lord, son, what did you do to the woman?"

"Besides steal seven grand, gamble it away and humiliate her in an Amarillo honky-tonk?" Jack grimaced as he climbed into the passenger seat. The wound in the back of his head had required six stitches and still hurt like hell, despite the local anesthetic. Or maybe that was just his conscience.

"And now you have to go retrieve your truck from her backyard."

"Well, technically, it's just down the road."

"Any chance she'll key the paint job and slash your tires?"

Before seeing Mara again, Jack would have said no. But she had changed in the past four years. Drastically. "Let's just hope she got her revenge by leaving me wounded to fend for myself."

Riley's side-eye glance was a thing of sarcastic beauty. "Poor you."

"Seriously, Riley, a big man dressed in camo attacked her right there at her cabin and she didn't want to call the cops." Jack shook his head and immediately regretted it as the stitches pulled, sending a stinging pain through his scalp. "What the hell is going on?"

"Maybe you should call the local cops and make a report," Riley suggested. "The guy assaulted you."

"Technically, I attacked him first."

"Because he was attacking your friend."

"Who hates me and doesn't want the police involved. What if she lies and says I assaulted someone?"

"Wow, you really don't trust her, do you?"

"I broke her trust. She owes me nothing."

"Then maybe you should just get your truck, follow me back to town and let's get on with our fishing trip."

Jack could tell by Riley's tone that he didn't like what he was saying any more than Jack did. But he was right. Mara Jennings didn't want him anywhere near her life, and he sure as hell couldn't fix what he'd broken.

Still, the idea of leaving her out here to fend for herself went against every instinct he had.

He'd half expected to find his truck had been towed away, but the Ford F-150 was still sitting there on the side of the narrow gravel road, about thirty yards from the cabin's driveway. Mara's little blue Mazda car wasn't anywhere around, however.

Had she gone back to work?

As Jack opened the passenger door of the Bronco, Riley asked, "Should we expect you at dinner?"

Jack turned to look at his brother-in-law. "I don't think so."

Riley's mouth flattened to a thin line, but he didn't look surprised. "Be careful, Jack."

Jack nodded and closed the door, walking slowly across the crunchy gravel to his truck. He settled in the driver's seat and put the key in the ignition. But he didn't start the truck.

Instead he settled down to wait.

HER CELL PHONE rang while she was loading the data sanitization programs on the computers she had to leave behind. She glanced at the display. Alexander Quinn.

She ignored the call and shoved the lone laptop computer she was keeping into her backpack. She'd packed light for the bugout. She wasn't exactly a clotheshorse to begin with, and the less she had to carry with her, the better to make a complete escape.

It might be a relief, really, to go underground again. No more pretending to be someone she wasn't.

Someone she never had been.

The phone rang once more. Quinn again. With a grimace, she answered the phone. "What's up, boss?"

"What happened to Jack Drummond?"

"What happened?" She should have known he'd already heard about the visit to the urgent-care clinic. Purgatory was a small town, and not much went on there that Quinn didn't know about. "He fell down the porch stairs and split his skull on the gravel. He's fine."

Although she couldn't say that for sure, could she? She'd left him at the clinic to fend for himself.

"Fell down the steps?"

A flutter of alarm twitched through her gut

as she realized maybe Quinn knew something she didn't. "Yes. Why? How do you know about what happened?"

"Someone saw you with Drummond at the clinic."

She bit back a sigh. Damn small towns. "I didn't want him to sue me. Or, more to the point, you, since this is your property."

"And he just fell down the stairs. Unaided?"

"You think I pushed him?"

"Did you?"

"No. I didn't." It was a grizzly of a camouflage-clad intruder who did the pushing, she added silently. "And I made it clear to Drummond that I don't care to see him again."

"I've looked into Jack Drummond's past," Quinn said.

That fast? She glanced at her watch. Nearly seven. There were no windows in the secret room, but the day had already been waning before she finished packing. She would be out of daylight when she finally hit the road.

Maybe that was better. Easier to disappear in the dark.

"Not curious?" Quinn asked when she didn't respond.

"Not particularly." A lie, of course. Curiosity was one of her most enduring traits. And one that often got her into considerable trouble.

And Jack Drummond was, if nothing else, an intriguing creature in all the wrong ways.

"He's been off the rodeo circuit for two years," Quinn said. "Retired after a bull ride gone wrong crushed his pelvis. He's lucky he can walk."

She hadn't noticed any sign of infirmity. But she supposed she wouldn't have. She'd been trying very hard not to pay any attention to Jack Drummond at all.

"Is there a point to telling me this?" she asked.

"He used to have quite the reputation as a hard-drinking, hard-loving, hard-riding cowboy."

She knew his reputation had been well earned. She knew that better than most people did. "Used to have?"

"Four years ago, he stopped drinking. I don't know if he stopped womanizing, but the stories about his bedroom exploits subsided around that time. The only thing he kept doing was riding, and from what I hear, he became increasingly reckless about it, which led to the accident that ended his career."

Four years ago, Mara had walked into an Amarillo honky-tonk to meet Jack for a date and found him wrapped around a pretty blonde barrel racer he'd met while waiting for Mara to arrive. He'd been three sheets to the wind already, and when he spotted Mara, he'd just smiled a drunken smile and shrugged.

Just shrugged, as if to say, what's a cowboy to do?

God, she hated him for that.

She'd never believed for a second that he'd change. Not for a second. Men like Jack Drummond barreled their careless ways through the world, leaving destruction in their wake, and almost never suffered the consequences.

"Maybe he just hides it better now," she said.

"Maybe," Quinn conceded. "Or maybe something happened to change his behavior."

She knew what he was suggesting. She'd never told him about what had happened in Amarillo, but Quinn was smart enough to guess.

"I don't care," she said flatly, looking at the duffel bag lying at her feet. She didn't intend to stick around Purgatory for another hour, so what Jack Drummond had or hadn't done four years ago meant nothing to her.

Nothing at all.

"Why do I think there's something you're not telling me?" Quinn asked.

"Because you're a suspicious old spook," she snapped back. "Go bother someone else." She ended the call, her hands shaking.

Stop, she thought, forcing her hands to go still. She took a couple of long, deep breaths, tried to clear her mind of the clutter that Jack Drummond's unexpected invasion of her life had wrought.

The data-shredding programs she'd fed into her remaining computers were nearly finished. Anyone, Quinn included, who tried to figure out what she'd been working on would fail.

The information she needed to continue her work was saved on three portable flash drives sewn into the padding of her backpack, safe enough for the moment. Once she reached her next bolt-hole, she'd try to find a safer place to keep them.

It was time to leave Mara Jennings behind for good.

Chapter Four

Darkness fell across the woods surrounding Mara Jennings's cabin, aided by lowering clouds that cocooned the cabin in a misty veil. Rain had not yet started to fall, but the air outside the truck was cool and damp with the promise of precipitation when Jack got out to stretch his legs.

Nothing had stirred around the cabin for a couple of hours. No cars had passed his parking place going in either direction. He checked his watch as he climbed back into the truck—not even eight o'clock yet.

Where the hell was she?

Suddenly, light flickered on inside the cabin.

Jack sat forward with a start.

A dark silhouette glided past the one window Jack could see from his vantage point. It was hard to make out distinguishing characteristics like height or shape, but he supposed it might have been a female.

Had Mara been in the cabin this whole time?

Or had an intruder made his way inside without Jack seeing him?

He'd unpacked his Colt pistol and loaded it while he was waiting for something to happen. He checked it now, making sure he had a round chambered, and reached for the door handle.

The light in the cabin went off.

Jack froze in place.

A second later, the front door opened and a dark-clad figure slipped out onto the porch. It crossed to the steps and began to descend, coming out of the shadow of the porch roof.

Despite the darkness of the cloud-covered night, Jack's eyes had adjusted enough to the low light to make out Mara's pretty oval-shaped face as she lifted it toward him.

She froze in place when she spotted his truck.

He knew she probably couldn't see him sitting there in the cab, watching her. Maybe she'd just assume his brother-in-law drove him back to the hotel for the night and they'd pick up the truck in the morning.

After a few more seconds of complete stillness, Mara edged toward the tree line to her left, closer and closer to the woods. If she entered the dense thicket of trees and underbrush, he'd lose sight of her completely.

Would that be so bad?

"Yes," he whispered, the hiss of breath loud

in the quiet truck cab. It would be bad, because the woman was clearly in trouble. Someone had tried to attack her that afternoon and now she was sneaking out of her house with a duffel bag and a backpack and disappearing into the woods. After dark.

What the hell was going on with her?

Gunfire split the silent mountain air, impossibly close. Ducking on instinct, Jack peered through the truck's passenger window, his heart rate tripling in the span of a few seconds.

Was she shooting at him?

A rustle of bushes caught his attention just before Mara raced onto the road in front of his truck. A second shot rang out as before, and Mara halted with a jerk. She pitched forward, disappearing from his view.

Jack's heart stuttered as he scooted toward the driver's door, jerking twice at the door handle before he managed to get it open.

Keeping low, he moved toward the front of the truck and peered around the bumper.

Mara lay facedown on the gravel, her eyes half-open and her breath coming in harsh gasps.

For a second, Jack wasn't sure what to do. He might consider himself a man of action, but most of the action had to do with planting his tail on the back of an enormous, angry bull and trying to stay there for eight seconds. He was a pretty good shot with the Colt pistol gripped tightly in his right hand when he was standing at a shooting range with nothing else going on, but he'd never been shot at in his life.

"Mara?" he whispered, looking for blood in the dark gravel beneath her body.

In the woods to his right, the whisper of movement in the bushes spurred him into action. Scrambling forward, he grabbed Mara by the upper arms and dragged her around the truck. She struggled weakly against his grip, but he managed to get her tucked between him and the door of the truck.

"Where were you hit?" he asked quietly, daring a quick peek over the bed of the truck.

"Are you with him?" she asked in a raspy growl.

"What?"

"The man with the gun—are you with him?"

Jack heard more movement in the woods. A lot closer this time.

Without taking time to answer her, he moved her to the side and pulled open the door of the truck. "Can you get in?"

Her eyes met his, glittering in the dim glow of the truck's dome light. He felt her wriggle against him, the slide of her body against his sending an unexpected, badly timed flood of heat pouring into his groin. She turned around, the curve of her bottom brushing against him and sparking more fires as she scrambled into the truck cab ahead of him. "Get us out of here."

He pulled himself behind the wheel and turned the key. The truck growled to life.

"Is there a faster way out of here than backward?" he asked.

"No."

"Hold on." He put the truck in Reverse and hit the gas pedal. The Ford truck jerked backward, spraying gravel as he braked, spun the steering wheel into the resulting slide and whipped the truck into Drive, shooting forward.

Beside him, Mara's hands gripped the dashboard as she struggled to keep from tumbling onto the floorboard. "Go!" she rasped.

Another gunshot rang out. Jack heard the screech of metal on metal and realized the last shot had hit the truck. He swallowed a profanity and pressed the gas pedal to the floor.

"Left or right?" he asked seconds later, forced to brake when they reached the T intersection with the winding road that had brought him there from the main highway.

"Left," she said after the briefest of hesitations.

Right would take them to the highway, he knew. He wondered where she was taking them.

He watched the rearview mirror as he barreled

along the narrow two-lane road that appeared to hug the curvy contours of Deception Lake. Riley and Hannah had taken him fishing there earlier that morning, he realized, though probably on a different part of the lake, since nothing about this road or these woods seemed familiar to him.

He spared a quick look at Mara. "Where are you injured?"

"My pride," she answered in a hard, flat tone.

"You were shot."

"My duffel took the bullet. It knocked me down and winded me, but I'm not shot."

He wasn't sure he believed her. In fact, he was beginning to wonder if he could believe a single thing she'd said to him since they ran into each other at the diner a few hours earlier.

"Who was shooting at us?"

"Us?" She looked at him from beneath the tangled fringe of her auburn bangs, wide-eyed and rattled.

"I'm pretty sure there's a bullet hole in my truck, so yeah. Us."

"I don't know."

She was lying. At least, she wasn't telling the whole truth. Maybe she didn't know exactly who'd ambushed her in her cabin or who had started taking potshots at them from the woods.

But she had a theory, one she had no intention of sharing. He could hear the secret hiding in her voice.

Fine. He could table his curiosity a little longer, while they got as far away from the gun-wielding maniac in the woods. But as soon as they found a safe place to stop and regroup, he was going to ask a lot more questions.

And she was damn well going to answer them.

BY THE TIME they reached the point where the lakefront road ended in a T intersection with another highway, the rain that had been threatening all afternoon hit with a vengeance, pelting the truck and limiting visibility to a few dozen yards. The highway at this end of the lakefront road was the main artery leading from Purgatory to the little mountain hamlet of Poe Creek about fifteen miles north.

Like Purgatory, Poe Creek had never managed to become a tourist destination as so many little towns in the Smokies had, but its close proximity to the mountains as well as a main road to Douglas Lake ensured that there were a handful of hotels and motels in the area, including several small, cheap places where a few bucks could get the night clerk to look the other way when you rented a room with cash and no identification.

She directed Jack to head north, shifting her

duffel bag to her lap and setting the backpack on the floorboard at her feet. She took time to buckle her seat belt—the last thing she needed was the Tennessee Highway Patrol to flag them down for breaking the state's seat-belt law. "Can you belt yourself while driving?" she asked.

Jack shot her an incredulous look. "A little busy trying to see ten feet in front of the truck at the moment."

"Hand me the buckle and I'll do it for you." She knew, in the greater scheme of things, seat-belt safety laws were way down on the list of things she needed to worry about at the moment, but doing something—anything—that would restore a sense of control was a good thing in her book.

Jack passed the seat belt across his lap and shoulder, and she took the buckle he held out to her, pulling it down into place and connecting it with the latch at his hip. Her fingers brushed his thigh as she finished, making the skin of her knuckles tingle where they'd touched the denim-clad warmth of his muscular leg.

She pulled her hand back into her lap and grabbed the duffel bag, inspecting the hole that had ripped through one end of the sturdy canvas.

"Are you sure you weren't hit?" Jack shot another worried glance her way.

"Positive." She made herself look away from

his dark eyes, a little unnerved by the attention. She'd spent most of the past few years of her life cultivating an aura of invisibility, making herself as unobtrusive and unremarkable as possible—a complete turnaround from her first twenty-three years of life, when all she'd craved was attention and she'd gone out of her way to find spectacular, outrageous ways to make it happen.

She'd learned the hard way that the wrong kind of attention could be downright deadly.

"Where are we going?" Jack asked.

She didn't like the way he used the word *we*, as if he thought he was any part of what she had planned. For all she knew, he was involved in this whole mess she'd managed to land herself in the middle of. How could she be sure that he just happened to be there, picking up his truck, at the moment she tried to make her escape and ran into another camouflage-clad man on a mission, this time carrying a rifle?

She couldn't be sure it was the same man who'd accosted her on the porch of her cabin. Neither could she be certain he wasn't.

In short, she didn't know who was after her. Or why.

Though the "why" part of the equation was pretty limited. Either it was the project she'd been working on for Alexander Quinn that had drawn unwanted attention to her, or it was something from her past rising to bite her again. Either way, she had to get as far away from Purgatory as she could, as fast as she could.

And she had to do it flying under the radar, which meant the last thing she needed slowing her down was a cowboy with no idea who she was or what kind of unholy mess he was swaggering into.

"Not going to answer?" he asked, sounding incredulous.

"Just go until I tell you to stop."

The look in his dark eyes should have given her plenty of warning, but she still found herself slamming forward into her seat belt as he whipped the truck onto the shoulder of the road and put it into Park.

"I realize that I owe you money and an apology for the things I did, but that goes only so far." Jack spoke in a low, twangy growl that reminded her of a week she'd spent in Wyoming when she was just eighteen, partying with frat boys who'd taken her along for their spring break trip out West. She hadn't even been attending the university where frat boys had been students; they'd picked her up at the little diner where she'd been working part-time as a waitress and brought her along for the ride.

That she hadn't been left raped or dead in Jackson was a miracle; sure, the frat boys had tired of her quickly when she wasn't willing to be shared around the group, but at least they hadn't forced her to do anything. They'd just abandoned her to find her own way back to school in Massachusetts, and thanks to a very nice cattle rancher and his wife, she'd managed to scrape up enough cash for the bus ride home.

The cattleman had spoken in the same low, slow Western drawl that Jack had just used, with the same dark tone of sad disapproval. She felt herself folding in on herself, like one of those hard-shelled armadillos she used to watch amble across the backyard of her childhood home.

"I don't know where we're going," she answered.

"And you're not going to tell me who we're running from."

"I don't know that, either."

Neither of her answers was a complete lie. She wasn't sure where he'd be going once she ditched him. And she wasn't sure whether the man who'd accosted her that afternoon was the same man who'd shot at her tonight, or what his exact reason for targeting her might be.

So many reasons came to mind.

"We should get back on the road," she said after Jack sat silent for another long moment. "We're sitting ducks on this shoulder."

"Which brings me back to the question, where are we going?"

"Poe Creek," she answered.

"And that's where?"

"North on this highway."

His lips thinned to a grim line as he put the truck in drive and eased back onto the highway. "I wish I'd just taken your advice and given that seven grand to charity."

"Not too late," she muttered.

"You know damn well it is too late, Mara."

His words fell into a thick, tense silence broken only by engine noise, the squeak of the windshield wipers and the relentless drumbeat of rain on the roof of the truck. She kept her gaze angled forward, on the headlights cutting through torrents of rain that looked as if heaven's floodgates had all opened at the same time on this narrow stretch of four-lane highway.

The dashboard clock read eight-twenty. She'd left the house at five till eight. How was it possible that less than a half hour had passed?

"We should go back to Purgatory," Jack said a couple of minutes later. "My brother-in-law is a deputy sheriff in Alabama. He can help."

"No."

"Are you running from the police or something, Mara?" He asked the question with a hint of humor in his tone, as if he thought he knew her so well, knew that she couldn't possibly take one step over the line between right and wrong.

He didn't know her at all.

"I just don't want to involve anyone else in my problems."

"Too late for that, darlin'." There was that western Wyoming twang again, gravelly, deep and compelling, with just a hint of Texas at the edges.

She didn't let herself look at him. His voice was disarming enough. She didn't need to see the lean angles of his jaw or the dimples that played around the corners of his mouth when he smiled. She had a lifelong habit of falling for the wrong men, and she knew Jack Drummond was as wrong as it got. In so many ways.

Jack switched to the left lane and began to slow down. She sat forward in alarm. "What are you doing?"

"Turning around," he answered as he swung the truck into a U-turn and headed toward Purgatory.

"Jack, no. Please." She reached across the seat and grabbed his arm.

He shot a look at her. "What are you so damn afraid of, Mara?"

"Please, let's just go to Poe Creek like we planned."

"Like you planned. I wasn't consulted. And

you won't tell me what's really going on here. Besides, my truck, my way."

"Then let me out. I'll walk."

"In the pouring rain." Skepticism edged his voice. "For miles."

Before she had a chance to come up with a response, the rain-washed road visible ahead in the truck's headlights took on an eerie red glow. A minute later, she spotted red flashing lights on the road ahead, coming from multiple emergency vehicles.

Sinking a little lower in the seat, she peered through the windshield, trying to see through the rain to get a better idea of what was happening on the road ahead.

"Accident?" Jack murmured.

It was hard to make out their exact location in the driving rain, but she thought the vehicle ahead must be pretty close to Salvation Bridge, which crossed Black Creek about a mile outside Purgatory's tiny downtown district. As Jack slowed to a stop behind a couple of other vehicles that had been ahead of them on the road, she could just make out the back of a tractor trailer rig lying on its side.

"Truck jackknifed," she said bluntly as one of the cars ahead of them pulled a U-turn and started back in the other direction. "Must be blocking the whole bridge."

"Is there another way into town?" he asked as he and the car ahead of him pulled forward to where a Tennessee Highway Patrol officer was making sweeping arm gestures to indicate they should turn around, as well. As she opened her mouth to answer, he slanted a hard look at her. "And would you tell me the truth if there was?"

"You know you can go back by the lake road," she answered, trying not to let her anxiety show. "If you want to risk driving past a guy with a rifle who knows what your truck looks like."

His mouth tightened, but he didn't reply.

A few moments later, they passed the turnoff to Deception Lake, and she let herself breathe deeply again.

Jack broke the silence a couple of miles farther up the road. "What's the plan, Mara? Since you're getting your way, the least you can do is let me in on it."

"There are motels there. It's on the way to a lot of tourist destinations that stay booked up, so the extra motels help ease the overbooking situation."

"And motels are going to solve your problem with the gun-toting crazy person how?"

"I need a safe place to think."

"To think. Think about what?"

About ditching you, she thought, keeping her

expression neutral. "About who could be doing this to me."

Jack was silent for so long she couldn't keep from taking a peek at him. He was staring forward through the windshield, his eyes narrowed and his lean jaw set like stone.

"What?" she asked when the silence between them stretched to the snapping point.

He slowed the truck and pulled over onto the shoulder again. His gaze turned to meet hers, and in the dim glow of the dashboard lights, his eyes were as black as midnight. When he spoke, the words came out in a low rumble. "Who the hell are you?"

Chapter Five

Jack wasn't sure what he'd meant by the question he'd just asked, but the expression that flitted across Mara's face at his words sent a queasy sensation through his gut.

It had been sheer, unadulterated terror.

Her expression shuttered almost immediately, replaced by a stony facade as impenetrable as the rainy night. "You know who I am."

No, he thought, *I don't.* "You're very different from what I remember."

"People change." One shoulder gave a delicate shrug. "A lot has happened in the past four years."

"You lost your sister."

"Yes." The cool stone expression didn't waver, but in her eyes he caught a flicker of something that might have been pain.

"I'm sorry I never got to meet Mallory."

"She wouldn't have liked you anyway." She

turned her gaze forward, as if she could actually see through the rain-streaked windshield.

He couldn't hold back a soft laugh. "I imagine not."

"We shouldn't keep sitting here on the side of the road," she said after he said nothing more. "We should find somewhere to stay for the night and then we can talk in the morning."

He had the distinct feeling that if he took his eyes off her for more than a minute, she wouldn't be around in the morning.

Would that be so bad? he wondered as he pulled the truck back onto the highway. She'd clearly been on her way out of town when she ran into the man with the gun, and who could blame her? She'd already been accosted. And earlier, she'd run into the man who'd not only broken her heart but emptied out her savings account. He was damn lucky she'd never pressed charges, although technically, she'd consented to his borrowing the money.

He'd just lied about why he wanted it, and when he'd lost it all—and lost her faith in him that horrible night in an Amarillo bar—he headed out of town and left her to pick up the pieces.

He hated thinking about that time of his life, hated what he'd done. What he'd become. Maybe he'd never really loved her the way she'd loved him, but he'd known she was a special person, someone who certainly hadn't deserved any of the hell he'd brought into her life.

She deserved to be happy, and she wasn't. She deserved to be safe, and instead she was being threatened and hunted for reasons he couldn't fathom. What had the sweet, simple Texas girl he'd known back in Amarillo gotten herself involved in?

He had to know. He had to help.

And then, maybe, he'd feel as if he'd finally paid his debt to her.

When they came upon Poe Creek several minutes later, the little town seemed to rise out of the rainstorm like an abandoned ship suddenly cresting the waves of a churning sea. Central to the small town square was the alabaster-front town hall, gleaming pale and pristine in the truck's headlights. Their reflection off its gleaming exterior cast a ghostly glow on the scene that sent an unexpected tremor through Jack's gut.

"The motels start showing up just down the road." Mara's husky voice broke the tense silence in the truck. "The better places will probably be booked up already—there's always some sort of festival or another going on around here during the spring—but we can probably find a couple of rooms at one of the seedier places."

She was only partially right. The first three

places he stopped were completely booked up, and at the fourth place, a boxy two-story brick building with a flickering sign out front proclaiming it to be the Mountain Hideaway Motor Lodge, the bored desk clerk informed him there was only one room left, but it offered two beds. "Best I can do," she said through a stifled yawn. "The Smoky Mountain Arts and Culture Festival is this weekend."

Two beds was better than nothing. It wasn't as if either he or Mara was exactly a seething bundle of uncontrollable lust, right? They could handle sharing a room until morning.

"I'll take it."

He paid with cash, and the clerk didn't ask for any ID, so he didn't offer any. He supposed that would allow them to remain anonymous and hidden, at least until morning.

"One room?" Mara looked at him as if he'd just stolen another seven grand from her when he told her about the room.

"Like you said, some sort of festival in the area. Arts and crafts or something."

"I hate festivals," she growled.

"Since when? You used to be a festival fanatic."

Her cool blue gaze flicked up to meet his. "A lot has changed."

"I guess it has." He reached for her duffel bag

and backpack, intending to carry them to the room for her.

She pulled them more tightly to her and shook her head. "I've got them." She opened the passenger door and dropped lightly to the pavement of the parking lot below.

"Room 126," he said as he dashed behind her to the walkway that ran the length of the first floor. The walkway for the second floor provided cover from the rain, and as Mara walked ahead to their room, he took the opportunity to shake some of the rain off his hair and clothes. His Carhartt waterproof jacket was probably a little warm for a Tennessee spring, but the rain rolled right off him, dripping to the concrete walkway beneath his feet.

He could've used the Stetson he'd left in his hotel room, however.

He wondered what Riley imagined him to be doing right now. Probably nothing as remotely strange as what he was actually doing, he realized, a grim smile curving his mouth as he used the key the clerk had given him to unlock the motel room door and let himself and Mara inside.

There were two beds, as promised. But that was about all the furniture there was in the room.

"On a scale of one to hazmat level four, how bad do you think the bed linens are?" Mara dropped her backpack on one of the beds and cast a baleful gaze in his direction. "This was really the only room available in town?"

"That's what the clerk said."

"He probably just wanted your business."

"She. And if she wanted our business so much, she'd have given us two rooms like I asked."

For a second, Mara slanted a look his way that reeked of suspicion.

He frowned. "You think I asked for one room on purpose?"

She didn't answer, but her own brow furrowed in response as she looked down at the duffel bag she'd dropped on the floor at her feet.

"God, Mara. I know you think I'm a complete ass, but manipulating situations like this has never been my style. You know that."

Her lips pressed tightly together, as if she were trying very hard not to throw a retort back at him. Mara had never liked confrontation. She had never really fought back. She'd certainly never bristled with fury the way she was doing at the moment, her rain-curled hair a deep, shimmery red in the harsh motel room lighting and her eyes blazing cobalt-blue, as if her anger had sent electrical charges racing through her body, sparking explosions wherever they met resistance.

He felt an answering energy coiling low in his

belly, a jolt of pure sexual adrenaline that caught him entirely flat-footed. He'd wanted Mara during their time together, as he would have wanted any attractive, available woman. But he'd never felt anything quite as intense as the potent wave of desire that rolled up his body to settle in the center of his chest like a blazing ball of fire.

Maybe he was just reacting to her unexpected fury. But whatever it was shooting sparks through his nervous system, it was making the tiny hotel room feel considerably smaller.

He dug into the pocket of his jacket and pulled out a couple of packs of crackers he'd bought from the rickety vending machine in the motel office. "Cheese or peanut butter?"

She dropped wearily onto the bed closest to the door and looked up at him through a lock of hair that had fallen halfway across her eyes. "Cheese." She bent and pulled the duffel bag up on the bed beside her, examining the single bullet hole visible in one corner of the bag. "I guess it wasn't a through-and-through after all," she murmured, her complexion going pale.

He quelled the urge to sit on the bed beside her and give her a comforting hug. "Anything damaged in there?"

She unzipped the duffel and dug through the contents, pulling out a folded pair of socks that had been ripped by the bullet. "Seems to be the only thing." Digging around a little more, she came out with a misshapen slug. "And here's the culprit."

The sock must have slowed the velocity of the projectile, he guessed, trying not to dwell on how badly the situation might have gone if the assailant with the rifle had made a better shot.

He sat across from her on the second bed. "Are you sure you're okay?"

Her eyes flickered toward his without meeting them. "I'm sure."

"And you have no idea why someone's targeted you?"

She kept her gaze averted and shook her head.

He didn't believe her, but he decided pushing her on the topic wasn't going to solve anything. Maybe she just needed time to decompress. Time to feel a little safer, a little less hunted.

Meanwhile, he had no desire to eat a pack of crackers without something to wash them down. The drink machine in the motel office had been out of service, but he had a cooler full of iced soft drinks in the back of his truck that he hadn't yet unpacked from their morning of fishing.

He handed her the pack of cheese crackers and started toward the door. "Be right back."

He felt her gaze on him but forced himself not to look back at her as he left the room and dashed through the driving rain to the truck. He hauled the cooler from the bed of the truck and had started back toward the motel room before he remembered that he had a bag of dirty clothes stashed in a plastic garbage sack in the backseat of the truck cab. He might be able to find something clean enough to wear the next day, at least until they could hunt down a laundry.

He stopped short, ignoring the rain sliding beneath the collar of his rain jacket. *Hunt down a laundry? Just how long are you planning to spend running with this woman, Drummond?*

A flash of lightning lit up the sky, thunder crashing within a couple of seconds. The loud boom propelled him away from the truck as fast as he could run while burdened by a cooler full of ice and drinks and a plastic bag of dirty clothes dangling from his rain-slick fingers.

He spotted a glimpse of Mara's face between the motel room curtains before she disappeared from view and the door to the room opened. He hurried inside to put the cooler on the floor. Tossing the plastic bag next to it, he stepped outside again long enough to shake the rain off his jacket.

"What's this?" Mara asked, gesturing toward the cooler.

"Beverages," he answered, pulling up the top to reveal that the unseasonably warm March day hadn't managed to melt the ice surrounding about a dozen cans of soda.

She eyed the drinks with a slight scowl. "Don't suppose you have anything stronger? After the day I've had—"

"I don't drink anymore, Mara."

Her gaze snapped up to meet his. "Oh. Sorry. I didn't realize."

"It's okay. I don't expect you to do the same. But no, I don't have anything stronger."

She flattened her lips briefly before bending to pull out a Sprite. "Thanks. Those crackers were about to choke me."

He grabbed a diet ginger ale and picked up the bag of dirty clothes, carrying them with him when he crossed back to what appeared to be his bed for the night, since Mara was sitting in the middle of the bed nearer to the door.

"What's in there?" she asked around a mouthful of cracker crumbs as he untied the black plastic bag.

"Don't get too close or you can probably smell them," he warned with a faint smile. "I remembered I had some dirty clothes in the truck. I'd meant to look for a laundry in town, but I got… sidetracked."

Her lips quirked in what almost passed for a smile. "There's probably a laundry here in Poe Creek."

"Yeah." He set the bag of clothes aside, turning his full attention to her. "Which brings up a question. Just how long do you think we're going to be here in this lovely little burg?"

She looked down at her half-eaten package of crackers. "You can leave whenever you want."

"And you're going to what? Walk out of here on foot?"

"That wouldn't be your problem."

He set aside the package of peanut butter crackers and turned to face her, leaning forward to close some of the distance between them. "It's my problem. I'm not leaving you here to fend for yourself."

Her gaze came up then to meet his, curiosity battling with suspicion. "I'm nobody to you. I never was." There was no emotion behind the words, not even regret. Just a calm statement of fact.

And she'd never seemed less like the Mara Jennings he'd once known than she did in that moment.

The hair on the back of his neck lifted, sending prickles of sensation spreading across his flesh. He picked up the package of crackers lying unopened on the bed beside him and toyed with the plastic wrapper. "Do you remember the night we spent camping up at Lake Meredith? It was June, wasn't it?"

Her gaze darted toward him without quite connecting. She shrugged. "What about it?"

He put the crackers back down and rose, crossing the narrow distance between the two beds until he stood beside her, towering over her. He leaned forward, caging her with his presence but taking care not to touch her. "Remember how hard it rained that night? Just like tonight."

Her eyes narrowed as they rose toward him. Her chin jutted forward, sharp as a spear. "Your point?"

He closed the distance between them, waiting for her to move away from him. Or push him away.

Anything but what she actually did, which was reach out with one small, strong hand and grab the front of his T-shirt, pulling him forward until he lost his footing and landed sprawled across her.

Oh, hell.

Even as Jack's lean body fell across hers, even as her pulse skyrocketed and raw desire flowed hot and sweet through her veins, she knew she'd made a terrible mistake. She'd promised herself that sex was off-limits. Men were off-limits. And sexy men were most definitely off-limits. They made her crazy and reckless and stupid, and she'd had about all she could take of crazy, reckless and stupid for one lifetime.

But when Jack's hips aligned with hers, and she felt his body respond to the sweet friction, she curled her fingers more tightly in his shirt and lifted her gaze to his.

His face was so close she couldn't focus on his eyes. So she gazed at his lips instead, the soft, full lower lip and the narrower upper lip, the way they trembled apart when she splayed her other hand against his rib cage and let it wander over the contours of his narrow waist until her fingers tangled in the waistband of his jeans.

His breath heated her lips, and he paused, so close, so tantalizingly close. She felt his hesitation, his confusion, and a part of her brain that wasn't swimming through a haze of need tried to coax her to push him away.

But Jack chose that moment to move himself, not away but closer, his hands sliding to her thighs, urging them apart to fit himself more perfectly against her.

His mouth covered hers with no hesitation, no preamble. Just a hard, hot kiss that made her blood sing and her mind reel.

In the annals of her long history of bad decisions, this was turning out to be the worst ever.

And she couldn't bring herself to give a damn.

She wrapped her legs around his lean hips and

drove her fingers through his hair, anchoring his mouth to hers. She parted her lips and answered his passion kiss for kiss. He was hard in all the right places and soft in unexpected places, like the almost delicate way his tongue explored hers, as if tasting her, testing the sensations, drinking in every drop of her desire.

When he let her go and rolled away, the loss of his body against hers was a visceral shock. For a breathless second, she couldn't move, couldn't think, could only feel a strange emptiness she couldn't explain or even define.

The bed moved, rocking her where she lay. Jack sat up, his back to her, his shoulders hunched forward as he rested his elbows on his knees and took several long, deep breaths.

She dragged her gaze away from his broad, muscular back and looked up at the ceiling, hating herself. Hating him for making her want something she knew would be nothing but a disaster.

Hating him for pulling away from her before she got a chance to dive into that disaster head-first.

She felt him move, felt his gaze on her. It glided over her in exploration, as tangible as a touch. She closed her eyes and still felt his scrutiny stroking lightly over her whole body.

When he spoke, it was barely more than a

whisper, just audible over the drumbeat of rain outside the motel room. "I knew something was wrong. *You* were wrong."

Her heart skipped a beat.

"Look at me." His voice solidified. Deepened. When she didn't open her eyes immediately, he spoke again, his tone hard and unforgiving. "Open your damn eyes and look at me."

She complied and found him staring at her, his narrowed eyes sharp. His expression was unyielding and absolutely devastating.

"You didn't remember that I owed you seven thousand dollars. Hell, you barely even recognized me at all. I know it's been nearly four years, but I haven't changed that much." He pushed one long-fingered hand through his hair, lifting spiky black tufts that her own fingers itched to smooth back into place. She clutched handfuls of the nubby bedspread to keep her traitorous hands to herself.

"I was distracted," she said. The words sounded weak and unconvincing, even to her.

"A guy in camouflage grabs you, and before I can even reach you, you've extracted yourself from his grasp and gone for a gun." He shook his head. "But you hate guns. You hate violence. Or you did."

"My sister was murdered."

"I know." A bleak look turned his brown eyes ebony. "I know your sister was murdered."

She started to rise, but he caught her arm, holding her in place.

"Then earlier. You wanted a drink. But you never drink. You hated when I drank, remember?" His eyes narrowed. "I suppose you're probably going to tell me that things change. People change. Especially after a traumatic experience. Right?"

"It's true," she said faintly.

"Except when it's not." He let go of her arm, his gaze daring her to move. She lifted her chin, refusing to budge, and the dark look in his eyes melted into regret. "I told myself that very thing. I've been thinking it all day, trying to put everything into some kind of order that made sense, but nothing really fit. Until you pulled me down on this bed and showed me something I didn't think you had in you."

He knew. She stared back at him, her pulse roaring in her ears.

He leaned closer, his heat flooding her yet somehow unable to drive away the hard chill that washed over her at his next soft words. "You're not Mara, are you? Mara's the woman who died that night in Amarillo. Which means you're—"

"Mallory," she finished for him, dread and relief rattling through her in equal parts. "Yes.

But you're wrong about one thing. Mallory Jennings died that night, too. And she can never, ever come back."

Chapter Six

Mallory's words hung in the air between them, a ghostly echo in the silence. Jack struggled not to drop his gaze, not to look away from the raw fear and pain he saw blazing back at him in her wide blue eyes.

"What happened?" he asked softly, not sure he wanted to know.

"They thought she was me. So they shot her twice in the head and set the house on fire." She broke eye contact, her gaze dropping to her lap, where her fingers twisted together like nervous spiders.

"Who were they?"

She shook her head. "That *is* the question, isn't it?"

"You don't know? Not even a guess?"

She took a deep breath and let it out on a long sigh. "Lots of guesses. But no proof."

"So you took Mara's identity to save your own skin."

She blanched at the question, her gaze whipping up to his. "You don't get to do that, Jack. You have no right to judge me after the things you did to Mara. So you can go to hell."

Anger flared in his chest. He tamped it down ruthlessly. She was right. He had no right to judge anyone else's behavior after the things he'd done, the mistakes he'd made. "Did you know she was in danger?"

Her gaze dropped again. "I knew it was possible, but I wasn't sure—I thought it would be safe enough to go back there for a visit. It was Christmas. I'd already spent so many Christmases away from home."

"Why was it possible someone wanted to hurt you? What did you do?"

"Why do you think I did anything?"

"You're not the only person Mara told her secrets to."

Warm color rose up her neck, into her cheeks. "Trust me, she didn't tell you even half of it. She was far too kind for her own good."

He couldn't argue with that assessment of Mara Jennings. "So, tell me, what did you do this time that put you on somebody's hit list?

"I don't have to tell you anything. You're not a cop and you're not my lawyer."

"I'm the guy with a truck that can get you out

of here if things get worse. You might want to be a little more cooperative."

Her jaw squared. "I don't need you."

He put one finger under her chin and tipped her face up, forcing her to meet his gaze. "Yes. You do. There is someone out there who wants you out of the way. They've tried to kill you at least twice, including today."

"That's why I was trying to get out of town tonight."

"And go where?"

"I'm not telling you that. Or anyone else. I trust no one but myself."

"That's a piss-poor way to go through life."

"You'd know about that, wouldn't you?"

Well played, he thought. "I don't have an agenda here, Mallory. I thought you were someone I'd hurt, so I wanted to make it up to you. That's all. And since we're here, and we're both sort of in trouble at the moment—"

She shook he head. "*I'm* in trouble. You're just along for the ride, for reasons I sort of understand. But now that you know I'm not the woman whose life you wrecked, you can go."

"Mara loved you."

Mallory's blue eyes filled with tears, but he could see her steel herself against them, refusing to let them fall. She blinked a couple of times and held his gaze. "I know that."

"I didn't get to tell her how sorry I was for the many ways I hurt her. I'll never get to. But I can help her sister, so let me. Please let me help you."

"Out of guilt? I'm not sure that's a good reason."

"Mallory—"

"Or maybe you're hoping that little tango we did here on the bed was just a preview?" She edged closer, her voice softer and sexier, but the deep blue of her eyes had hardened like ice. The bitter edge of her voice sliced right through his chest. "Bet you've never had the chance to compare twins in bed before, have you?"

"Mara and I never slept together."

She pulled back, her eyes narrowed as she seemed to search his face for any signs of deceit.

"She was different from other women." He looked away, feeling branded by the sheer force of her wary gaze. "And it's not that I didn't try. Believe me, I did."

"But she played by the rules." Mallory's voice was barely more than a whisper.

"I should have known I'd hurt her. I've never played by the rules in my life." He might have cleaned up his act these days, but deep down, he was still that rebellious kid from the Wyoming sticks, who'd hated his hard-nosed father and loved the hell out of his sister. He had to look no further for proof than where he was right now, sitting in a cheap motel with a dead woman he'd come damn close to bedding just a few minutes earlier.

"She never hated you. She wouldn't even let me talk bad about you." Mallory shrugged. "She just didn't have it in her, I guess."

"But you do."

Her eyes slanted toward him. "Yeah. I do."

"Then I guess maybe you're the one I need to apologize to." He turned to face her fully. "I'm sorry I wasn't better to your sister. I hurt her and took advantage of her, and I could sit here and give you excuses for why I did and what kind of person I was then, but it wouldn't change the fact that I treated her very badly. And I will go to my grave regretting that I never got the chance to say those words to her."

"What am I supposed to do?" she asked after a long, tense moment of silence. "Grant absolution or something? So not my style."

"You don't have to do anything." He stood, needing distance from her. But there was no way to get away from himself, and he was the author of the shame and disgust burning a hole in his gut.

He crossed to the motel room window and pushed aside the stiff canvas curtain. Outside, the night was inky, rain and cloud cover vanquishing any hint of moonlight. A lone lamp shone at the far end of the parking lot, near the motel office. There was another tall lamp on this end of the motel, but the bulb was dark.

The parking lot was full, he noticed. It seemed the clerk hadn't been lying about being booked up.

"Mara said you lost your own sister." Mallory's voice was close. He felt the whisper of her breath on his neck. "She was murdered, too, wasn't she?"

He turned to look at her. She stood little more than a foot away, her arms folded around her as if she were cold, even though the motel room was well heated. Quelling the urge to wrap his arms around her and warm her with his own body, he pulled his jacket from the chair where he'd draped it and offered it to her.

She looked inclined to refuse, but after a second's pause, she reached out for it. Rather than hand it over, Jack circled her and helped her into it, barely resisting the urge to smooth the sleeves down her arms and tuck the collar around her neck.

"Nice coat," she murmured. "Cost much?"

"Enough," he answered. "You have a mercenary streak?"

"I like nice things. Is that a crime?"

"Depends on what you do to procure them."

She turned her head to look at him. "Just what exactly did Mara tell you about me?"

He couldn't help smiling, despite the bleakness of his current mood. "Only nice things."

"You're such a liar."

"Well, she might have mentioned how much she worried about you. Said you never could seem to be happy."

She passed her hand over her face, her gaze dipping away.

"I never answered your question," he said as tense silence unspooled between them. "Yes, my sister was murdered."

"And you never found out who did it."

"Actually we did. Almost four years ago." Right around the time Mara had died, he realized. "Emily finally got justice."

"But it didn't bring her back." The forlorn tone of Mallory's voice made his gut ache.

"No, it didn't." He missed Emily every day.

Mallory crossed slowly to the motel bed and sat down. She hunkered deeper inside his rain jacket, letting it swallow her whole. "Sometimes I grab my phone and start to dial her number, just to say hello, you know? I get her number all the way in the speed dial before I remember she can't answer."

He eased closer, sensing that despite her introspective mood, she might still be inclined to bolt if he spooked her. She reminded him of a mustang he'd once tried to break. The filly had been as wary and wild as she was beautiful, and she'd fought him every step of the way, even though he'd seen in her liquid brown eyes a yearning to make a connection.

He'd never saddle-broken her, but she'd stayed on the ranch where he'd worked, too bonded with him to follow the herd back into the wild. She'd died during a difficult foaling not long after Emily died. Already eaten up with grief, Jack had cried for days—for his sister, for himself and for that headstrong, beautiful mare.

He saw a lot of that wild mustang in Mallory Jennings at this moment. And he felt an old, familiar tug of kinship that scared the hell out of him.

"It's late and it's been a hell of a day. Why don't you try to get some sleep?" He crossed to the window again to give her a modicum of privacy.

He heard the rustle of fabric, the sound of a zipper. He closed his eyes, dismayed but not surprised when his body responded to the sound of her shedding clothes for the night.

Long minutes passed while he stood gazing out into the rainy night and waited to hear Mallory's breathing slow and steady, but she seemed restless, the bedsprings creaking as she tossed and turned.

He finally turned back toward the bed and found her watching him, her gaze narrowed and wary. "Something wrong?" he asked.

"What's *not* wrong?" she asked, her shoulder rising in a halfhearted shrug. She was still wearing her pale gray T-shirt, but her jeans lay rolled up on the end of the bed, and she'd folded his jacket and laid it on the other bed before crawling under the bedcovers.

"We're warm and dry. We're safe, for now."

She didn't say anything in response, so he crossed to the other bed and sat next to his coat. She'd rolled onto her side, her gaze following him as he leaned toward her, resting his elbows on his knees.

"I get that you don't like me or trust me. But I'm actually a pretty good guy to have around when there's trouble." He shot her a lopsided smile. "I'm just foolhardy enough to take a bullet for someone else, so there's that, right?"

The corners of her lips quirked upward, just a bit, then a reluctant smile broke out across her face like sunshine, making his gut tighten with desire. "So I guess you're not completely useless, then."

"Get some sleep. Tomorrow we'll figure out what to do next."

She nodded slowly and closed her eyes. This time, her breathing slowed and grew even within a few minutes.

Jack eased off his boots and set them quietly on the floor beside his bed, pulling his cell phone out of his pocket. Fifty percent power. He'd left his charger in the hotel room back in Purgatory, but he could charge it on the vehicle charger in the morning.

He checked for text messages. Three from Riley; he'd left his phone on vibrate and had apparently missed the texts during the wild rush out of town. All three were a variation on the same question: had he lost his bloody mind?

He sent a text message to Riley, assuring him he was safe and would be in touch. As he did so, another text message came through, from Hannah this time. He read it once, then again, his tired brain mulling through the new information. Then he shut down the phone to save power and stretched out on the bed, rolling onto his side so he could see Mallory Jennings in the dim golden light from the lamp on the small table that sat between the beds.

The rain and her exertions had washed away what little makeup she'd donned that day, making her look years younger than she had when he'd seen her in the diner in Purgatory earlier that day. If any of Mara's oblique references to her sister's life had come close to the truth, Mallory had lived a harder life than her more settled twin, but whatever struggles she'd known hadn't seemed to take a toll on her youthful vibrance.

He wondered what kind of life could have led her here, to this little motel in the middle of nowhere, holed up with a virtual stranger and running in fear for her life.

And what kind of man had he become, that being here with her, with almost no idea of who she really was, what kind of trouble she was in or where they were going next, was the most exhilarating feeling he'd experienced in a long time?

THE ACRID TANG of burning wood seeped into her car through the air vents long before she turned the corner on Cottonwood Street and saw the little white clapboard house aflame.

It was the closest thing she had to a home. And her sister had been sleeping inside when she sneaked out earlier that night.

She parked the car haphazardly in the driveway and raced up the walk, her heart pounding with each frantic step. The door was unlocked; Mara never locked it. Mallory had warned her that the world wasn't safe enough for unlocked doors anymore, but Mara never listened.

"Mara!" She pushed through the thick, chok-

ing smoke, dodging the licking flames spreading quickly from the curtains now fully engulfed by fire to the furniture starting to incinerate from the inferno.

She almost stumbled on the body where it lay, still and oddly twisted, as if she were a doll someone had tossed to the floor and left to lie as it fell, arms and legs awkwardly turned, her head rolled to one side.

Her blue eyes were half-open. Unseeing. Blood pooled beneath her head, and long before her fingers touched the still vein in Mara's neck, Mallory knew her sister was dead.

Head shots. Double tapped. She'd seen it before.

She'd prayed to God she never would again, but God hadn't answered that prayer, either.

She started back toward the door, where Mara's purse lay on the table in the entryway. As she grabbed her sister's purse and started to dig for her phone, she stepped out onto the porch, seized by a painful coughing fit.

Her face felt damp. Reaching up, she felt tears sliding down her cheeks. Her knees grew wobbly and she stumbled toward the porch steps, grabbing the rail to keep from falling. Sitting with a thud on the top step, she opened Mara's purse and looked inside for her cell phone.

What she found first was her sister's wallet.

Mallory opened the wallet and found her sister's face, eerily identical to her own, staring back at her from a Texas driver's license.

When they were young, nobody had been able to tell them apart, she remembered. Then Mallory had changed her look, changed her attitude, changed her whole life, really. While Mara remained the same.

Mallory had changed her own look to match her sister's on this most recent trip home to Texas. She'd done it deliberately, needing the connection with her twin that they'd once had, that intensity of sisterhood that time, distance and Mallory's own foolish choices had never quite been able to obliterate.

And that need for a connection, that need to change herself back into her sister's twin again, had gotten Mara killed.

There was no doubt in her mind. Those bullets had been for her.

And now someone very dangerous thought she was dead.

Mallory stood slowly, holding on to the rail for strength. And maybe for a little courage, too. With her sister's purse and identity clutched firmly in hand, she descended the steps and walked back to her car.

The fire raged on, and Mallory waited as

*the world around her grew sooty and smoth-
ering, until everything light extinguished from
her world.*

MALLORY BLINKED SLOWLY, disoriented by the
sudden inky blackness surrounding her. She was
lying on her back, on a mattress. The faint tang
of disinfectant mingled with a whiff of mildew
and a darker, richer smell of leather and spice.
Tears dampened her cheeks; she dashed them
away with her fingertips.

Then she heard breathing, deep and even.
Masculine. Somewhere nearby.

Jack Drummond.

The lingering images of her dream faded, and
the heavy thud of her pulse quickened as she
remembered where she was and why she was
there.

She hadn't had a chance to get online to check
the status of her latest query, and she sincerely
doubted this fleabag motel had free Wi-Fi. Or
any Wi-Fi. Not that she'd trust it anyway. She
could create a hot spot with the burner phone
she'd bought in case she ever had to bug out and
leave behind the phone Quinn had given her as
part of her job. She couldn't afford to let him
track her with the company phone.

But she'd have to wait until she could get

hunkered down somewhere and get her own system set up.

She needed to get out of here. Get away from Jack Drummond and his big brown eyes, lean cowboy body and that delicious leather-and-spice smell still lingering on her shirt where his body had flattened her into the mattress.

Easing off the bed, she grabbed her rolled-up jeans and slipped them back on, hunching with her back to Jack to keep the sound of her zipper from reaching his ears. Her tennis shoes were still damp, but she pulled them on anyway, not wanting to take the time to dig in her duffel for a drier pair.

She picked up the duffel and her backpack and had started toward the door when she realized she might not get another chance to go to the bathroom for a while. Dropping the bags on her bed, she made a quick stop in the bathroom, not even bothering to turn on the light.

Coming back out into the darkened motel room, she stepped quietly past Jack's bed, not letting herself look at him. She needed to get out of there fast. The farther away she could get while he slept, the better.

The floor creaked as she neared the door and she froze in place, her heart rattling wildly for a couple of seconds. She heard no sound of movement coming from the beds behind her, however, so she eased her hand around the doorknob and gave a slow twist.

As the door latch clicked open, a hand closed over her wrist, and Jack Drummond's low voice hummed in her ear.

"Going somewhere?"

Chapter Seven

The scent of her, a delicate hint of flowers and something spicy, hit him like a two-by-four in the gut, and he had to struggle to keep his anger from dissolving into blazing desire.

"Let me go," she said in a low tone edged with desperation.

He released her arm but didn't move away, keeping her pinned in the narrow space between the door and his body. "Where did you plan to go?"

"If I wanted you to know that, I'd have told you." She stood very still, not looking at him, barely even breathing.

"I'm not your enemy."

"Then why are you keeping me captive?" she shot back, her gaze snapping up to meet his. In the faint light from outside that filtered in through the edge of the window drapes, her eyes glittered with anger and something else.

Fear.

He took a step back, gave her space to breathe.

She sucked in a deep breath and let it out on a sigh. "I need to get out of here."

"Away from me, you mean."

She didn't deny it.

"If you leave, I'm going to follow you."

Her brow furrowed. "Why?"

"Because you're in trouble. And you're Mara's sister, and I know she loved you." He shoved his hands in the pockets of his jeans, feeling strangely vulnerable. He didn't like the feeling. "I owe her."

"I don't need saving."

"You need someone to watch your back while you do whatever it is you've got up your sleeve. I can do that."

She cocked her head, her eyes narrowing. "What I have up my sleeve?"

"Mara once told me you were a computer whiz. Genius level. And that makes me wonder what you were doing carting lunch back and forth to a PI agency. You could be running their IT section, couldn't you?"

"How do you know I'm not?"

"I don't, I suppose." He glanced at the duffel bag and backpack still hanging over her shoulder. "Computer whizzes don't travel without a computer. Is yours in there?"

She clutched the strap of the backpack more tightly but didn't answer.

He stepped closer, lowering his voice. The air between them recharged immediately, like turbulence fed by a brewing storm. "While I was waiting outside your cabin, my sister-in-law was doing a little bit of snooping of her own. See, she knows your boss, Alexander Quinn. They've apparently crossed paths a few times. And he owes her and her family for some things they've helped him out with in the past."

Mallory's lips flattened to a thin line, but she didn't speak.

"She sent me a text earlier." He couldn't stop himself from leaning closer, erasing the distance he'd put between them moments before. "Quinn stopped by your cabin after we left. And whatever he found inside alarmed him enough that now he's got people out there looking for you. And me."

"Maybe you should let them find you," she murmured, her gaze dipping to his mouth. Her own lips trembled apart, her breath quickening.

Answering heat flooded his body. "I told you. If you go, I'll follow."

"You're crazy." Somehow she was even closer to him, her breasts brushing against his chest. He didn't know if she'd stepped closer or if he had been the one to close the distance.

He didn't really care.

"I rode bulls for a living," he answered, sliding one hand around to press against her spine, tugging her closer. "Crazy's baked into that cake, sweetheart."

She slipped her hands under the hem of his T-shirt, her fingers cool against his skin. She traced his muscles and the ridges of his rib cage with a light, maddening touch. "I don't need you."

"I think maybe you do." He bent his head and nipped at her jawline with his lips, eliciting a soft hum of pleasure from her throat. The sound vibrated through him to settle low in his groin.

"Only for this," she growled before she pushed him backward.

He stumbled, falling backward onto the bed. Sprawling there, he gazed up at her as she stood over him, realizing she could make a run for it before he could scramble up off the bed.

Even as he pushed himself to a sitting position, ready to take chase, she moved toward him, shoving him back down on the bed. Straddling his hips, she bent to kiss him. Fiercely. Hotly. All tongue and teeth and scorching lips and roaming hands.

She dragged his T-shirt up his body, scraping her short nails over his abdomen hard enough to leave his skin tingling. There'd be marks in the morning, he thought, and the image stoked his desire to a whole new level.

He wrapped his hand around the back of her neck and rolled over so that she was pinned beneath him, her body soft and welcoming as he settled between her thighs. Even in the darkness, he could see the gleam in her eyes, the faint glint of light reflected off her feral smile. The desire to take her was overwhelming. His mind was already three steps ahead of the rest of him, already buried inside her, moving within her, staking claim.

He was quickly losing control, something he could ill afford to do with a woman like Mallory Jennings.

He rolled off her, pushing away her hands as they clung to hold him in place. Crossing on shaky legs to the door, he leaned against the hard surface and flicked the light switch, flooding the small motel room with a bright golden glow.

He wished he'd left it dark, for the sight of Mallory still sprawled on the bed, her hair mussed, her breath coming in soft gasps and her eyes drunk with desire, was almost enough to unravel the last strands of his control.

"Why didn't you run?" he asked.

Her eyes narrowed, the desire fading into cool calculation. "And miss my chance to ride a genuine cowboy?" Her light Texas twang deepened. "Where's the fun in that?"

Her tone was flippant, but in those cobalt eyes he saw a feral desperation that echoed in his own chest. She wanted to escape. But not from here.

Not from him.

"Let me help you," he said, even though it was the last thing he'd intended to say. "Trust me."

Her eyes closed. "I can't."

"Why not?"

"Because you're not trustworthy." Her eyes snapped open. "And even if you were, I've learned the hard way not to trust anyone."

"Is that why you're even running from Alexander Quinn?"

She sat up slowly, straightening her shirt so that it covered her bare midriff. As the T-shirt hem skimmed down to cover the waistband of her jeans, the light revealed a detail he hadn't seen in the dark—a small silver hoop pierced through the skin of her navel.

How he'd ever mistaken her for Mara, he couldn't imagine. About the only thing the two women had shared in common was their DNA.

"I realize the man your sister described to you was not trustworthy. But I'm not that same man."

"Just because you supposedly stopped drinking?" She stood to face him, all long legs and messy hair, temptation personified. "How long since your last drink, cowboy? A month? A year?"

"Four years." It had been hard for the first year, easier as time passed and he didn't slide back into old habits. He couldn't say he wasn't tempted at times, but he'd managed to stay strong and sober so far, and as long as he never let himself think he was totally cured, he had a chance of staying clean for good.

"Well, good for you." She said the words flippantly, but he didn't miss a hint of surprise in her voice, or the grudging look of admiration in her eyes. "I never manage to kick a bad habit for more than a few days." Her lips curved in a wry smile. "Which probably explains my throwing you on the bed and trying to get into those jeans."

"You're really going to have to stop saying things like that." His voice came out in a growl.

The smile widened. "So you haven't kicked all of your addictions, then?"

"Stop trying to change the subject, Mallory." He put out a hand as she took a step closer. "What are you into? Is it illegal?"

"No." There was a hint of hesitation in her voice that made him doubt she was telling the whole truth.

"Unethical?"

"No." Her feral smile had faded into a wary frown. "Jack, if I tell you what I'm doing—" She stopped short, her expression pained. "People's lives are at risk. I'm trying to—" She stopped again and turned away.

"Trying to what? Save them?" He pushed away from the door and moved closer. "Protect them?"

She darted a quick look at him out of the corner of her eye. "Me? Do something altruistic? Didn't you listen to anything Mara told you about me?"

"She loved you. She had a lot more faith in you than you seem to have in her." As soon as he said the words, he knew they were harsh and unfair, and Mallory's flinch confirmed the fact. "I'm sorry. That was a low blow."

She pushed her fingers through the messy auburn waves of her hair, as if to tame the locks. She didn't quite succeed, but when she turned to face him, her expression had settled into a cool mask of indifference. "I don't really care what you think of me."

"I care what you think of me." He really did care, he realized with some dismay. "I want you to let me help you. I need to do it."

"Penance?"

"I suppose."

She looked at him then, really looked at him,

her narrowed gaze sharp enough to cut. He tried not to squirm under her sudden, intense scrutiny as he wondered what she saw when she looked at him.

A washed-up cowboy without a clue what to do with his life now that his days on the circuit were over? A former drunken womanizer who'd broken her sister's fragile heart? The stubborn jerk who stood in the way of her own escape plans?

He was all three, he knew. But he couldn't change the past, and he sure as hell wasn't going to let her hare off into God only knew what kind of danger by herself.

"You're serious, aren't you?" she asked. "About trying to help me."

Something in her expression had changed. There was a softness in her eyes, a hint of vulnerability that made the world shift beneath his feet. He stood very still, waiting for her next move.

"I'm looking for someone," she said finally. "Someone who doesn't want to be found. And if I don't find him soon, a whole lot of people are going to get hurt. Or worse."

"SHE SHREDDED THE hard drives. I'm not sure I'm going to be able to reconstruct anything."

Alexander Quinn quelled a flash of anger and

met Anson Daughtry's troubled gaze without blinking. "She must believe she's in danger."

"Then why didn't she contact you?" Daughtry dropped into the chair across from Quinn's desk, all long limbs and a deceptive somnolence that hid a quick, brilliantly twisty mind. "You should have let me have a go at the project. She was always too much a wild card."

"You keep my computer systems running. I'll handle personnel."

Daughtry's lips pressed tightly together, but he didn't argue.

"It's not in her nature to trust people. With good cause." Quinn rose from his desk and crossed to the window that faced east. Night and rainfall obscured the normally breathtaking view of the Smoky Mountains he enjoyed, but his memory supplied the image of softly rounded peaks carpeted with evergreens that made the mountains look as if they'd been upholstered in blue-green suede.

He'd left these mountains so long ago he could barely remember those boyhood years spent roaming the wilderness and imagining adventures far beyond the peaks and hollows of home.

But the mountains he'd always remembered, as if they were part of his flesh and bones.

Daughtry sighed audibly. "She left her phone at the cabin. Took all the insides out, so we'll have to contact the wireless company to get a call log."

Quinn had anticipated that turn of events. "Nick Darcy's already on it."

"Do you think she's gone rogue?" Daughtry asked.

Quinn turned to look at the younger man. "I guess that depends on your definition of rogue."

"That's not an answer."

No, Quinn supposed it wasn't. But it was the only answer he planned to give Daughtry. A life of lies and deception in the CIA had taught Quinn a lot of lessons, but the primary one was that there was no such thing as a trustworthy colleague. Every human being had a price, even the most honest and moral of people. Money, sex, family, love of country, love of self, even a passion for the greater good could be wielded like a weapon against any given person at any given time.

The secret was knowing which weapon to use against whom.

But life could not be lived in pure isolation. And limited trust had to be granted from time to time to limited people in limited ways.

He'd chosen to share a part of Mallory Jennings's secret with Anson Daughtry. Not the name of the elusive gray-hat hacker she'd been helping Quinn seek. But other than Nick Darcy,

Daughtry was the only employee of The Gates who knew their pretty office assistant was anything but an ordinary clerical worker.

Had even that partial information put her life in danger?

Or was she running from that troubled past that had brought her to Quinn's attention in the first place?

He didn't know the answer to Daughtry's question. And if there was one thing Alexander Quinn hated more than anything else in the world, it was not knowing the answer to a question that intrigued him.

Mallory Jennings had gone off the grid, and if Hannah Patterson's earlier call meant anything, she'd gone there with a mercurial, unpredictable former rodeo cowboy in tow.

He returned to his desk and sat, nodding toward the door. "Let me know if you uncover anything new."

Daughtry frowned, clearly not happy with being summarily dismissed. But he unfolded his lanky body and headed out the door without saying anything more.

Quinn waited until the door closed behind the other man before he released a sigh of frustration. He'd known she'd be trouble.

She always had been.

MALLORY WATCHED JACK'S reaction carefully, looking for any obvious tells. She'd gotten pretty good at reading people in her younger days—a matter of survival, really, given the kind of people she'd run with then. Nineteen and already finished with her undergraduate studies at the famed Massachusetts Institute of Technology— MIT—she'd been ready to run wild. It had been a short step from the tech nerds she'd shared classes with to the brilliant underworld of hackers with whom she'd eventually fallen in. The majority had been mostly harmless, their forays into the silicon nervous system of the world's computer networks all part of a game of cat and mouse with no real nefarious intentions.

But there had been others whose motives were anything but harmless. And naturally, being young and reckless, a headstrong little Texas redneck swimming in a murky pool of cyber-sharks, she'd gravitated to the thrill seekers and the rule breakers.

For all she knew, Jack Drummond could be one of them. She'd betrayed some very dangerous people when she went to the CIA with what she'd discovered about a plan in the works for a cyberterror attack that would have crippled the world economy for months, maybe years.

Jack Drummond had wandered into her sister's life within a few months of her first contact with Alexander Quinn. Had that been a coincidence?

The lean, handsome cowboy stared back at her, his eyebrows raised in a slight quirk. But if he knew what she was talking about, he didn't show it. "That's a bit dramatic," he commented.

He wasn't a hit man. Or even a hacktivist true believer, she decided when he continued to gaze back at her with frustration and a hint of skepticism. "I guess so. But it's also true."

He caught the back of one of the two chairs in the small motel room and pulled it closer to where she stood. He sat and looked up at her with earnest dark eyes that made her want to believe he was exactly what he claimed to be.

Her habit of trusting only herself had kept her alive so far. But for what? A life constantly on the run? Of always looking over her shoulder?

You tried to trust someone else, and your sister ended up dead.

"Are you a hacker?" he asked.

She released a deep breath. "Define hacker."

"You breach computer security systems, I guess. For Quinn?"

"No."

"No, you're not a hacker, or no, you don't do it for Quinn?"

"No, I'm not discussing this with you. And you know that not all hackers are criminals, don't you?"

He shoved his fingers through his dark hair in frustration. "You're changing the subject."

"No, I'm defining the terms. Yes, I'm a hacker. So was Steve Jobs. So is Linus Torvalds."

"Who?"

She almost laughed. "Cretin."

He shrugged, a smile flirting with his lips. "My interests are a little more…visceral."

Heat flooded through her veins. He really needed to stop being so damn sexy. He was making her insane. "Not all hackers are lawbreakers. There are basically three types—and as a cowboy, you should appreciate this—called white hats, gray hats and black hats."

"And you're a white hat?"

At the moment anyway, she thought. "In this instance, yes."

"But not always?"

"Not always," she conceded, shooting him a sharp look. "But we all have our sinful pasts, don't we?"

"We do indeed." The partial smile grew a little bolder, quirking the corners of his mouth. "So, this white-hat hacking you're doing—"

"It's not exactly hacking. Not what I'm doing

now." She hesitated, apprehension tying her gut into knots.

"You said you're looking for someone," he prodded. "And he's hiding somewhere in cyber-space?"

She'd told him that much? She closed her eyes, shutting out the magnetic pull of his dark gaze. "Jack, please."

"Not your secrets to tell?"

She shook her head. "And I wouldn't tell them, even if they were."

His voice lowered to a gravelly whisper. "What are you afraid of, Mallory? Can you tell me that much?"

"You," she whispered. She opened her eyes, steeling herself against the concern she saw shimmering in his gaze. "I'm afraid of you."

Chapter Eight

What they both needed, Jack thought as he stared out the window into the rainy gloom, was a hot meal and sleep, and not necessarily in that order. But he had no desire to venture out in the storm for whatever fast food they might be able to stumble across at this late hour, and sleep was proving elusive.

Mallory had blurted out her fear of him, then disappeared into the bathroom about a half hour ago. The shower had stopped running fifteen minutes after that, and there had been only silence since.

There was no window in the bathroom, and the only vent he'd noticed was far too small for a human to crawl through. So she was still in the bathroom, right?

He turned away from the window and crossed to the bathroom door, placing his ear against it. Hearing nothing through the flimsy wood, he rapped with his knuckles. "Mallory?"

"I'm fine." Her voice sounded thick and muffled.

"Are you going to stay in there all night?" He kept his own voice deliberately light. "Because I had a lot of coffee earlier today—"

He heard movement, then the rattle of the door handle. He stepped back as the door swung open and she glared up at him through red-rimmed eyes. "Are you happy now?"

He sighed. "Clearly you're not."

"I said I'm fine." She brushed past him, the herbal scent of her bath soap lingering as she passed. She'd changed into an oversize Green Bay Packers jersey and a pair of silky running shorts that revealed the well-toned legs her jeans had hidden.

Forcing his libido into submission, he followed, settling on the bed across from where she sat finger-coming her damp hair. "You said you're afraid of me."

"Forget I said anything about anything."

"Can't do that. You also mentioned a lot of people getting hurt."

"*Maybe* a lot of people *maybe* getting hurt."

"And that's supposed to make me feel okay about dumping you here at this fleabag motel and going back to my family vacation?"

A look of consternation furrowed her brow. "Yes. You're shallow and self-centered. Life is a game to you—I mean, my God, you ride bulls for a living!"

"*Rode* bulls."

"Whatever." Her eyes narrowed a twitch. "How long did it take to recover?"

"Almost six months."

She winced. "Bet the medical costs were hell."

"Considering how lucky I am to be alive, I guess they were worth it." He'd thought at the time he was a dead man, with that much weight on top of him, but the surgeons told him he'd gotten miraculously lucky. "The doctors said if the bull's weight had landed a few inches higher, I'd be dead."

She held his gaze without flinching at his words, but he could see a slight tremble around the corners of her eyes. Mara's eyes used to do the same thing when she was trying to hide her reaction. He'd seen it a lot during the last troubled days of their doomed relationship.

Maybe Mallory and her twin hadn't been as different as she seemed to think.

"I had saved up some prize money, and I had been smart enough to get insured through the rodeo cowboys' association, so I managed to get through the aftermath without taking too big a financial hit. I've been doing some freelance consulting since then."

"What kind of consulting?" Her expression

looked bored, but he heard a note of curiosity in her voice.

"Bull breeders, horse breeders—they like a pro cowboy's opinion on what breeding stock to purchase. Did some teaching at rodeo schools—"

"Rodeo schools?" She looked skeptical.

"I thought you were from Texas," he shot back with mock disapproval.

"Got the hell out as soon as I could." She flashed him the first genuine grin he'd seen from her since they met. It was breathtaking. Her sister, Mara, had always had a pretty smile, but Mallory's grin was all teeth and dimples and utterly infectious. He found his own mouth curving in response.

"I liked Texas." His smile faded. "For the most part."

"I hear a whole lot of the female part of Texas liked you, too." She arched one dark eyebrow. "Didn't you know Mara wasn't the buckle bunny type?"

"I knew she wasn't a groupie," he said. "But she was sweet. And smart. And she didn't even like the rodeo very much, but she liked me anyway."

"I don't think she was that surprised when you blew it."

"We weren't suited."

"No."

"But I took advantage of her kindness and her caring. Even when I knew it couldn't go anywhere." If he was honest with himself, he had never had a relationship he had ever thought could go anywhere. He'd resigned himself to spending the rest of his life moving from one relationship to the next.

"You humiliated her."

"I did. I'm sorry about that. I'm most sorry that she never got to hear me say so."

"Guess you don't remember that drunk call you made to her later that night, then."

He frowned. "What drunk call?"

"Apparently you were pretty maudlin. Begged her to forgive you, promised to stop drinking, told her she was way too good for you—"

"I didn't do that."

"She saved the message. Let me listen to it."

He eyed her suspiciously. "She wouldn't have done that."

Her lips quirked. "No, she wouldn't have. But she did say you called to say you were sorry. I take it you didn't?"

"Not that I recall. And I didn't get drunk enough to forget something like that."

She sighed. "That was Mara. Protecting your sorry ass even when you didn't deserve it."

He had a feeling she wasn't talking about him anymore.

Any hint of humor had left her face. "I don't know who killed her, Jack. But whoever it was, they were after me, not her. Do you have any idea how hard that knowledge is to live with?"

"No," he admitted. "But I know what it's like to lose one of the few people in the world who really gives a damn if you live or die. And I'm real sorry you do, too."

To his surprise, she reached across the narrow space between the hotel beds and caught his hand. "I believe you really are."

He closed his fingers around her hand. "Let me help you, Mallory. I don't have any agenda here. I swear. I just owe Mara for the things I did, and I know she would have wanted me to help you if I could."

Nibbling her lower lip between her straight white teeth, she gave him a considering look. Finally she took a deep breath and let go of his hand. "I'm looking for a hacker. Someone I knew once, a few years ago. He was a white hat at the time, but I'm not sure he still is."

"What's his name?"

"I don't know his real name. Quinn does, but he never told me. I just know the hacker name he used to go by when I knew him—Endrex. Quinn says he's also gone by pwnst4r and Phreakwrld." She spelled out the screen names for him.

"And what is this guy supposedly up to?" Jack

was reasonably technology-savvy, but the hacker underworld Mallory was trying to explain to him might as well have been on a different planet.

"That's what I've been trying to find out."

"You said before that a lot of people could get hurt."

She scooted back on the bed, curling one leg up under her as she leaned forward, her slender fingers toying with the nubby bedspread fabric. "There's been chatter."

"Chatter?"

"Cross talk. Rumors. Hints at something big coming. The people I worked with at The Gates seemed to think there could be a large-scale domestic terror attack in the works."

Jack's gut tightened. "And you're in the middle of this?"

She shot him a glare. "No, I'm not in the middle of it."

"But you're looking for a guy you think might be."

"He might be. Or he might be trying to thwart it. Quinn seems to think it's the latter, but—"

"But you don't?"

"I don't know. Being a white hat at one point doesn't mean he still is. And Endrex always had his own agenda, even when he was doing things for the government. I just never could figure out what that agenda might be, from day-to-day."

"How well did you know this guy?" Even as the words escaped his mouth, he realized they sounded like an accusation. Her gaze snapped up to meet his in response, and he gave himself a mental kick. "I mean, did you ever meet him in person? Or was everything on the internet?"

"The internet."

"So you don't even know if he's a guy."

"He's a guy. I knew people who'd met him. In the 'real world.'" She made quotation gestures with her fingers at his look of skepticism. "He's a guy. Midthirties by now. Longish hair. Believe me, I've been asking everyone I know online about him."

"Maybe you asked the wrong person the wrong question," he suggested. "Is there any way to track the people you talked to? See if you can figure out what triggered someone to send a rifle-toting goon after you?"

"Maybe." She made a face. "I've been a little busy running for my life and trying to get away from a mule-headed cowboy with a savior complex."

He couldn't stop a grin at her description of him. "Probably more a guilt complex than a savior one, but otherwise…"

She heaved a gusty, deliberate sigh. "Well, while we're sitting here playing name the complex, I'm losing work time." Mallory grabbed her backpack and pulled a sleek laptop computer from inside, setting it on the bed in front of her. Retrieving a power cord and a surge protector strip, she plugged one end into the computer and tossed the cord and surge protector strip to him. "Find a wall plug," she ordered, all business.

"Work time?" He crouched by the bedside table, grimacing as his old injury sent pain arcing from hip to hip. Finally locating the electrical outlet, he plugged in the surge protector strip and inserted the computer's adapter cord into one of the strip's slots.

"I need to find Endrex. I need to know if he's a good guy or a bad guy, and if the sudden interest from armed goons means anything, I need to find out sooner rather than later. So if you don't have anything helpful to add, just sit down, shut up and let me do my work."

He sat on the other bed, closed his mouth and watched as she attached a phone to a small adapter and plugged it into the laptop. He had no idea what she was doing or why she was doing it. And she clearly felt no need to enlighten him.

How he could ever have mistaken Mallory for her softer, sweeter twin, he didn't know.

HAVING THE KEYBOARD under her fingers again felt like downing a shot of whiskey, bracing her flagging spirits and calming her twitchy nerves.

She didn't bother with pulling out the flash drives that held most of her research notes—she'd resigned herself to letting Jack Drummond amuse himself playing bodyguard for the next little while, but she wasn't ready to tell him all her secrets. She'd already shared so much more than she'd intended, damn his sexy hide.

Instead she went by memory, cruising through several places on the Net where she might run into Endrex or someone who knew him. She didn't bother being subtle. By the time anyone could tunnel through all the layers of protection she'd set up to mask her identity and location, she'd be somewhere else posing as someone else.

Jack's idea of trying to track back through her connections over the past few days wasn't a bad one, though she'd never admit it aloud. She'd gotten into the habit of logging all her interactions with a program she'd written herself, and she'd dumped all the logs from all her machines onto one of the flash drives hidden in the lining of her jacket.

The question was, did she risk letting him see where she kept things hidden?

"Why'd you stop?" Jack asked.

She looked up at him, realizing she'd frozen in place as she was considering her options. She wasn't used to having someone watch her at the computer.

"Just thinking," she answered.

"About what?"

So much for shutting up. She shot him a pointed look. "About how to get away with murder."

He grinned, and her stomach turned a disconcerting couple of somersaults. "You want me to make myself scarce for a while?"

"Would you?"

"I thought I'd see if I could find a fast-food place that's open late. I'm starving." He pushed to his feet and leaned toward her. "You hungry?"

His low, intimate tone sent electricity zinging through her. She tried to appear unaffected. "Yeah. A burrito or something. And a Mountain Dew. Big as you can buy—I need caffeine."

He didn't move right away, remaining close enough that she could have lifted her face toward his and been within inches of kissing. Finally he straightened and stepped back. "Burrito and a Mountain Dew. Got it. What if the taco joint's not open?"

"Burger and a Coke. I don't really care." She shot him an exasperated look. "You're taking a long time to make yourself scarce."

"I'm reconsidering the wisdom of leaving you to your own devices."

"Sometimes, cowboy, you just have to take a leap of faith."

"I might find faith a little easier to come by if you hadn't already tried to ditch me more than once." He grabbed his jacket and shrugged it on as he headed out into the rainy night.

The room seemed bigger with Jack gone, but colder, too, as if the sheer force of him had filled the room with life and warmth. Mallory let her gaze wander to the door, wondering how long he'd be gone. Long enough to make another run for it?

He's addictive. You know the type—so bad for you, but you just can't resist one more taste. Mara's soft words rang in Mallory's memory. Her sister had been remarkably candid about the end of her relationship with Jack Drummond during their last, brief days together. She'd been past the humiliation stage, for the most part, and had settled into the sadder but wiser stage of a failed romance.

She'd been surprised by Jack's admission that he and Mara had never been lovers, though knowing her sister, she shouldn't have been. As Jack had said, Mara had lived by the rules. She wouldn't have been easy to seduce, either; where their troubled childhood had made Mallory reckless and wild, it had left Mara cautious and self-contained.

For identical twins, she and Mara had been opposites in many ways.

But apparently they'd shared a taste for lanky, mule-headed cowboys. Who knew?

If she was going to hightail it out of here before Jack got back, she'd have to make her move now. Pack up the laptop and accessories, walk down to the motel office and raid the vending machines for snacks to tide her over until she reached her next destination.

Wherever that was.

But the drumbeat of rain on the motel parking lot outside had a lulling effect, making her eyes droop and her limbs grow rubbery. She settled back against the bed pillows and pulled the laptop across her thighs, wandering in and out of forums and chat rooms she knew Endrex might frequent as she tried to coax herself into getting into gear.

He'd be back soon. Her chance to leave would be gone for the night.

And still, she didn't move.

Only the motel room door opening stirred her from her lethargy. A human silhouette filled the opening, blocking out the sound of the rain and the hint of light coming from the parking lot lamps. She couldn't make out features, only a nebulous darkness that seemed to writhe with mysterious life.

She tried to speak, but her voice betrayed her.

She tried to move, but she was immobile, as if her limbs had been nailed to the bed, holding her in place. Her heartbeat cranked higher, rolling like thunder in her ears.

The silhouette began to spread, filling the room like the impenetrable smoke that had overtaken the house where she'd left her sister's body burning. But there was no acrid odor, and the air around her remained cool and clean. A buzzing roar filled her ears, and in that roar she heard a whisper of sound, barely there and yet somehow inescapable.

"I'm everywhere. And nowhere." The relentless whisper flowed over her like a breeze, lifting the hairs on her skin. "And until you find me, you can't stop me."

Mallory woke with a start, her pulse still whooshing in her ears. Outside the motel room, the wind had risen, and lightning strafed the darkness, chased by ground-shaking booms of thunder.

Just a dream, she thought, trying to slow her breathing to normal.

But it wasn't just a dream. Not really.

Her laptop screen had gone dark. She rubbed her fingertip against the touch pad, and the image reappeared. She stared at the screen for a moment, the world tilting sideways as she read the rectangular chat box that had appeared in the middle of her screen.

There was one terse sentence typed within the box.

You found me.

Chapter Nine

Jack figured there was a fifty-fifty chance that when he opened the door to the motel room, Mallory Jennings would be gone. Maybe more like sixty-forty, he amended as he put the room key in the lock and turned it.

Or seventy-thirty. He pushed the door open and braced himself, prepared to find the room empty.

Instead he found himself staring down the barrel of Mallory's Smith & Wesson pistol.

He held up his hands, tightening his grip on the wet bag of food in one hand and the cardboard caddy holding their drinks in the other. "Don't shoot. I come with a food offering."

She released a gusty sigh and set the pistol on the bedside table. She looked rattled; he saw that as he closed the door behind him with his hip and approached the bed with no small amount of caution. "Burrito and Mountain Dew, as requested." As he circled the bed, he kept his eye on her, not liking the pale shade of her complexion or the worry lines carved into her brow. "Has something happened?"

"I don't know."

He set the drinks caddy and the bag of food on the bedside table next to the Smith & Wesson pistol. "Does that really mean 'I know what happened, but I'm not about to tell the idiot cowboy'?"

"No, it really means I don't know." She sat with her knees tucked up to her chest, the whole posture defensive. Her laptop computer sat closed on the bed next to her.

"Well, why don't you tell me what you do know?" He opened the bag of food and pulled out three foil-wrapped burritos. "You didn't say chicken, beef or bean, so I got one of each. I'll eat the ones you don't."

"Bean is fine." Her blue eyes slanted up to look at him. "That was thoughtful."

"I'm not a complete ass." He pulled the large cup of Mountain Dew from the caddy. "And this is as large as these fountain drinks come."

"Perfect." She put the straw he handed her in the cup and took a sip with a purr of pleasure that sent fire jolting straight to his groin.

He busied himself with his own food, trying to distract himself. What had they been talking about before her moans of pleasure drove his mind straight into the gutter? Oh, right. They'd been talking about whatever it was she didn't know. "What did you do while I was gone that's put you in such a state of confusion that you don't know what happened?"

"The syntax of that question has put me in a state of confusion," she muttered around bites of the burrito.

"I asked if something had happened. You said you didn't know."

She blew out a long breath, her brow creasing with frustration. "I stayed here instead of running out on you. Can't that be my concession for the evening?"

"Oh, we're going to keep score?" He put his own food back in the bag and leaned toward her. "Be careful with that, darlin'. Competition is one of my favorite things in the world. I do love to win."

She made a face at him. "So do I."

He was counting on it, he realized. It was why his blood was singing and his nerves were live wires. "What happened, Mallory?"

"Don't call me that," she said in a low voice. "For better or worse, I'm Mara now."

"I can't call you Mara. Sorry." He sat back, his appetite gone. "How about MJ?"

Her lips curved slightly at the corners. "My

mom used to call me that. My middle name's Jean. She'd call Mara MC for Mara Caroline."

"I didn't know that."

"We didn't like to talk much about our mom."

They were wandering pretty far off the topic of what had happened while he was gone that had left Mallory in such a troubled state, but his curiosity wouldn't let him drag her back to the current situation, not if she was willing to share something of her childhood. Even Mara, who'd been far easier to talk to than her prickly sister, had never spoken about her past in any depth.

He knew that she and Mallory had grown up in Lubbock, a couple of hours south of Amarillo. Their parents were both gone by the time he met Mara, and she spoke of them as if they'd been gone a long time.

"Your mother died when you were both young?"

"We were ten," Mallory said, her gaze directed toward the wall in front of her, though he could tell from the slightly misty expression in her eyes that she was seeing something from her past rather than the motel room's textured wallpaper.

"My mom died when I was a baby." He hadn't meant to tell her that nugget of information about his own life. He'd never even told Mara about his childhood in Wyoming, and she'd never asked.

He hadn't thought to wonder why, he realized, too grateful that she wasn't one of those women who liked to catalog a guy's whole life history as part of the dating experience. But maybe Mara had had her own childhood secrets she'd wanted to stay hidden. "I don't remember her. I just have some pictures."

"I don't know whether that makes you lucky or unlucky," she said flatly, her voice devoid of emotion. But he didn't miss the pain that etched tiny lines around the corners of her eyes. "Is it worse never knowing your mother? Or knowing her and losing her?"

He'd wondered the same thing for most of his life, until Emily died. At that point, he'd decided it was better that he hadn't ever known his mother, because he hadn't known what he was losing.

He missed Emily every single day of his life.

"How'd your mother die?" she asked.

"Car accident. What about yours?"

Her gaze snapped up to meet his. "My father killed her."

A chill rolled through him. "Oh. God, that's—"

"Horrible? Tragic?" She looked away. "Pathetic?"

"Mara never told me."

"Like I said, we never talked about her."

"Or your father."

She wrapped up the half-eaten burrito and put it back in the bag that still sat on the bedside table. "What's to talk about? He was a mean drunk and he beat her constantly. One day, he forgot to stop."

"I'm sorry."

She shrugged. "Not your fault."

"Who took you in afterward?"

"My aunt and uncle." She didn't elaborate, and Jack didn't see the point of prying further.

He'd been lucky, he supposed, that he and Emily had had their father, even if the old man hadn't exactly been the warm and fuzzy paternal sort. He'd kept them clothed and fed, made sure they got to school and did their homework. He'd even tried to find them a new mother a couple of times, but those relationships had never really worked out.

Jack had always figured the old man was just too hard to live with, but softhearted Emily seemed certain it was because their father's ability to love anyone fully had died with their mother.

"You weren't around, but I was," she'd told him more than once. "With her, he used to laugh and sing and tell jokes. When she died, it was like she took part of him with her."

Jack had never understood what his sister

meant until she herself had died, taking a part of him with her as well.

Pushing aside the old memories, he braced his hands on his knees and pinned her with his most unwavering gaze. "Why were you so rattled when I came in, MJ?"

She blinked, clearly thrown by the change of topic. "I wasn't rattled, exactly." She looked as if she were going to argue further, but then her shoulders slumped and she stretched forward to pull her computer back onto her lap. Releasing a deep breath, she scooted over and opened the laptop, a sideways nod of her head inviting him to join her.

Ignoring an insistent tug of desire, he sat beside her and looked at the computer screen. She was on a Windows operating system, he noted with surprise. He'd known a rodeo clown, a total technology geek, who'd sworn any computer freak worth his salt always chose Linux, but maybe the guy had just been blowing air up his chaps.

On the laptop's monitor screen, a couple of browser windows were open, and in front of them, a smaller window in the middle of the screen. On that smaller screen, there were three words typed in the otherwise empty box.

You found me.

"What does that mean?" he asked.

"I'm not sure." She crossed her arms, rubbing her hands up and down them as if she were cold. But the heater in the motel room was working well enough; if anything, it was a little warmer than Jack liked.

"You're looking for someone, and you get this message." He waved his hand toward the message box. "What had you been doing when it came in?"

"Wandering the Net. Places I'd met this guy Endrex before, years ago." She shrugged. "Half the sites are dead now, moved on to different places on the web or gone altogether. And I wasn't even trying that hard to find him. Mostly just messing around, thinking while my fingers played."

"You haven't tried to answer him?"

"Not yet."

"You think it's a setup?"

"I think it might be," she admitted. "Someone may be trying to lure me into a trap."

"Or it might be the guy you're looking for, trying to make contact." He shifted so that he could look at her. She turned her head and met his gaze, and he realized she was genuinely torn about what to do. Until this moment, she'd seemed almost militantly decisive. It was odd to see her at a loss. "If you're right about this guy, if he really is the key to keeping something very bad from happening, I think we have to take the chance."

"We?" She arched one auburn eyebrow, but in her blue eyes he saw a flicker of relief. Maybe she wasn't the tough girl loner she liked to pretend she was after all.

"I'm a bull rider who can no longer ride bulls." He leaned his head a little closer to hers, lowering his voice. "I need a little excitement in my life again. Let's take a chance here."

"What kind of chance?" she whispered.

The air between them charged instantly, and the earlier tug of attraction he'd felt turned into a relentless tide. There was a part of him that was certain she'd shifted the tone of their conversation on purpose, to distract him from his goal of helping her find this mysterious Endrex person.

The other part of him didn't give a damn what had motivated her. He just wanted to see how far she'd take her diversionary tactics.

All the way between the sheets?

He wrestled the reckless side into submission and eased back a few inches. "If there's a chance that typing an answer in that box there can stop people from dying, then I think you should do it."

Her gaze lingered on his mouth a breathtaking moment before it lifted to meet his. "There's a chance of that," she admitted. "There's also a chance it can get us killed."

"I'd call that an acceptable risk."

Her eyes narrowed as she considered his words. "There's that hero complex again."

"Believe me, I'm no hero. I just realized, once I sobered up long enough to take a critical look at my life, I've done nothing in this world worth telling my grandkids about."

"You don't think being a rodeo cowboy is interesting enough?"

"Interesting is not the same as worthwhile."

"And what makes you think you'll ever have grandkids?"

He smiled at her tart-toned question. "Because I want grandkids."

"And whatever you want, you get?"

"I could ask the same question of you, you know."

She dipped her head, her gaze wandering back to the laptop as if she had tired of the conversation. She gestured at the computer screen. "Since we're in this together, any suggestions about what I should say to this guy?"

Biting back a smart-ass answer, he considered the blinking cursor beneath the three word message. "He says you found him. Tell him you haven't yet, but you'd like to."

The look she darted his way was full of skepticism, but she typed in a terse reply. "Not yet. But I'd like to. Can we meet?"

For over two minutes, nothing happened. Then, as the tension in the room neared the snapping point, a new message blinked into view beneath Mallory's response.

"Resurrection Point."

Jack frowned at the screen. Why did that phrase seem familiar?

He glanced at Mallory, hoping the response meant something to her, but if it did, he couldn't see past the stony stillness of her expression to discern it.

She shut the chat window suddenly and snapped the laptop shut.

"What does that mean?" Jack asked quietly when she said nothing. "Resurrection Point?"

"I have no idea."

She was lying. She was a pretty good liar, really—her tone was just open and innocent enough to fool even a careful listener. But she'd already given away her agitation when she closed the laptop so suddenly, no matter how carefully she'd schooled her expression afterward.

"Then why didn't you keep chatting?"

She turned to look at him, her smile downright sultry as she leaned a little closer to him. "Come on, cowboy, don't tell me you never played hard to get."

"You think he'll contact you again if you ignore his message?"

"Wouldn't you?"

God help him, he probably would. But he clearly had a weak spot for redheads with a wild streak, especially one who was being deliberately provocative while sitting beside him on a motel bed.

Well, two could play that game.

He edged closer to her, daring her to move away. "Resurrection Point. Sounds like a place name."

"It does." She didn't move away.

He brushed his fingertips lightly against her spine, suppressing a smile at her swift intake of breath. "You've heard of it before, haven't you?"

She turned her head. Her lips brushed the ridge of his jawline. "I said I didn't know what it meant."

With each soft whisper of her lips against his skin, tingles of pleasure shot through him, pooling hot and heavy in his sex. He'd lost control of the situation the second she turned the seduction against him, he realized. He wasn't sure he cared. Losing this particular game of wills would probably feel a hell of a lot like winning.

She plucked at the buttons of his shirt, slipping the top two from the buttonholes and dropping a soft, hot kiss on the center of his chest. "You smell good," she murmured.

"So do you." He buried his nose in the cloud of auburn hair.

She unbuttoned the rest of his shirt, kissing each inch of skin she uncovered, until she reached the waistband of his jeans. As her fingers played teasingly over the button there, he caught her head in his hands and urged her back up his body until she was face-to-face with him again.

"Just how desperate are you to keep the truth from me?" His voice came out rough-textured, as if the strain of controlling himself had left every part of him scraped raw.

Hell, maybe it had. He wanted her so much right now he ached.

She closed her eyes to his scrutiny, and he felt the tiniest of tremors run through her before she answered. "I don't take anything seriously, remember? I'm sure Mara must have told you that much about me."

"I don't believe that." He eased her away from him and escaped to the other bed, bending forward to take several bracing breaths. His body raged at him for release, but for once, his brain won the battle.

Sex with Mallory Jennings now would ruin any chance of winning her trust. It would forever brand him as weak and unreliable in her eyes, because this attempt at seduction was nothing but a desperate power play, and if he fell for it, he was a fool.

"Can't stand the heat, cowboy?" Her soft taunt sent a shudder through him, but he held his ground, turning a cool gaze her way. Her blue eyes locked with his, but he was beginning to understand her body language tells. Her gaze was steady, but her lower lip was trembling, just the barest of quivers. He'd noticed it earlier, when she came out of the bathroom, red-eyed and trying not to show her weakness.

"I know you're scared, Mallory. I'm scared, too." He ignored the look of scorn in her eyes and concentrated on that quivering lower lip. "I know you only came with me because it was the fastest way to get the hell away from Deception Lake, but—"

A flicker of recognition darted through his brain. Something about Deception Lake, something he needed to remember.

"But?" she prodded when he didn't continue.

"Deception Lake. My brother-in-law and his wife took me fishing there this morning." God, had it been this morning, really? It felt as if a lifetime had passed since he was out on the mist-veiled lake, watching the sun rise over the mountains as he and the others pulled fat spring crappie from the lake.

"So?"

"I don't know if you do much fishing for crappie."

"I don't do much fishing of any kind."

"Well, in the spring, you fish for crappie in the flats, near brush and cover. In the fall, crappie relate to points. So we bought a map of the lake at the bait shop before we went fishing, so we'd know where to find the flats, but Hannah also marked all the points on the map, because she was hoping to come back in the fall."

"And?" she asked impatiently.

"One of the places marked on the map for good fishing was a place called Resurrection Point."

There it was. Her expression turned to stone—another tell. What he'd told her had struck a nerve again.

"We didn't go to Resurrection Point, of course," he added slowly, his gaze never leaving her face as he searched for more clues to what she was thinking. "The flats were across the lake on the western side."

"Is there a point to this fishing story?" she asked in a bored tone. But her gaze was sharp. Alert. She might be calm on the outside, but she was scared as hell on the inside.

"When I followed you home this afternoon, I remember thinking you were due east of where we'd ended up fishing this morning. And just now I remembered Resurrection Point was also due east of the flats. Which means that Resurrection Point is somewhere right around your pretty little cabin in the woods." He leaned a little closer. "Isn't it?"

"My pretty little cabin in the woods is *on* Resurrection Point," she snapped, the stone in her expression shattering to reveal raw fear.

"Which means—"

"Which means Endrex may have been the one who sent the shooter to kill me."

Chapter Ten

She'd made a mistake. Gotten sloppy. Trusted the wrong person.

Had she learned nothing in the past seven years?

"Tell me everything you know about this Endrex person." Jack's voice rumbled softly through the quiet motel room, like an echo of the thunder now rolling faintly in the distance.

"I know very little," she said.

"But you know more than you're telling me." Jack caught her chin with his fingers, turning her to look at him. She didn't want to meet his gaze, but those dark eyes compelled her. She felt a tug in the center of her chest, as if he had reached out, caught her heart in his fist and given it a little squeeze.

"I don't *know* anything."

"You suspect, then." He rubbed his thumb lightly across her chin, back and forth, the caress mesmerizing. "I know you don't trust easily. That's obvious. And you don't really know me. But—"

"But you're all I've got," she finished for him.

"Not exactly the ringing endorsement I was hoping for." His lips turned up at the corners. "But yeah."

Oh, hell, she thought, dipping her head away from his touch. She didn't want to admit it, certainly didn't want to put her life in his hands, but she needed his help. In less than the span of a day, someone had tried to kidnap her and kill her. Possibly two different people, if her brief glance at the gunman meant anything. He hadn't seemed as burly or tall as the man who'd accosted her at her cabin.

So at least two people with bad intentions were looking for her. Who might or might not be connected to the mysterious hacker named Endrex. And if it had been Endrex she'd been speaking with on the internet, he knew where she'd lived. He might even be behind the attacks on her.

God, her head hurt. Her eyes felt gritty and her gut rolled with a sensation somewhere between hunger and nausea. She needed sleep. Then maybe she'd have the brainpower to figure out some answers.

But how was she supposed to sleep when she felt as hunted as a mouse in a snake pit?

"Trust me, MJ." Jack caught her hand in his, caressing her knuckles with his thumb. "You've been afraid a long time, haven't you? You look so tired and hopeless."

"I want to trust you. I do." To her chagrin, her voice cracked.

"Then just do it." He came to sit beside her on the bed, his fingers twining with hers. "If you don't want to talk yet, fine. But don't bail on me. Let me keep watch tonight. You try to sleep. By morning, the storm will have passed and we can hit the road. Go wherever you want us to go."

Us, she thought, hating the word and clinging to it at the same time. It had been a long time since she'd felt anything but alone.

"Lie down. Close your eyes. Let me take care of you. Just tonight."

She found herself following his instructions, lying back against the pillows and sliding deeper beneath the bedcovers.

Jack pulled the blanket up, tucking her in as if she were a child, his expression so gentle she found herself wondering what kind of father he'd be. One who played with his kids, read them stories and dried their tears when they skinned knees or lost a ball game, she decided, comforted by the thought.

It was hard to reconcile the man sitting beside

her on the motel bed with her mental image of Mara's faithless cowboy suitor.

But Mara hadn't been a liar. What information she'd withheld had all been to Jack's detriment, she was sure. Every bad thing Mara had told her about Jack, the man himself had admitted, right?

But he'd also tried to make amends. Tried to pay back the money he'd stolen. He'd put his life on the line today to help Mallory, just because he felt he owed something to Mara's memory. The hard-drinking, womanizing cowboy of Mallory's imagination would never have done such a thing.

So which Jack Drummond was the real man?

ALEXANDER QUINN WAITED impatiently for the hotel room door to open to his hard knock. He heard the faint sound of movement from within, then the door opened a few inches and Riley Patterson's lean, weathered face appeared in the narrow gap, his blue eyes narrowed to sleepy slits. "Oh. It's you."

"May I come in?"

Riley peered at his watch. "It's after midnight."

"It's important."

"My wife and kid are asleep."

"Not your wife," came a grumpy female voice from the darkness within the hotel room. Hannah Patterson's pretty face appeared behind her husband's shoulder. "What do you want, Quinn?"

"I think you know."

Hannah grimaced. "Have I told you how much I hate that cryptic hogwash you fling around?"

"I'm looking for your brother-in-law."

"Yeah, good luck with that." Riley started to close the door.

Quinn stopped the door with his boot. "Jack is in danger."

"From you?"

Quinn suppressed a sharp reply, though Riley Patterson was starting to annoy the hell out of him. "There's something you need to know about the woman your brother is trying to protect."

The bored expression on Patterson's face shifted subtly, his blue eyes sharpening with interest. "Who?"

"You think her name is Mara Jennings. You think she's the woman your brother-in-law was seeing in Amarillo, Texas, four years ago." Quinn lowered his voice. "You'd be wrong."

"She's an imposter?"

"Of a sort." He nodded toward the door. "If you'll let me come in, I'll be happy to elaborate. I don't think this is a conversation that needs to take place in the middle of a public walkway."

"Oh, for God's sake, let him in," Hannah growled. "Let's get it over with, because I know him. He's not going to go away."

Quinn suppressed a smile at Hannah's frustrated drawl. "She has a point."

Patterson stepped back and let Quinn enter the hotel room while Hannah crossed to check on their sleeping son. Tucking him more tightly under the covers, she turned to face Quinn and her husband. "Keep it quiet, okay? He had an exciting day, and it took forever to coax him to sleep."

While she turned on the bedside lamp, casting a warm glow over the hotel room, Quinn pulled up one of the two chairs flanking the small table by the window and sat. Patterson and his wife settled on the edge of the bed, close to each other. Both were dressed for bed, Patterson in boxer shorts, no shirt, while Hannah had donned a simple cotton robe over whatever she was wearing underneath. Her shapely legs were bare from the knee down, including her feet. Her toes were neatly manicured and painted neon green, the sight making him quell another smile.

"What's the big secret about Mara Jennings?" she asked impatiently. "If she's not the woman Jack knew, who is she?"

"Mara's sister."

Patterson frowned. "Jack said Mara's sister died four years ago."

"Her twin sister," Hannah said, her green eyes sharpening as she made the mental leap. "Identical twins, right? DNA profiles would probably be indistinguishable without specialized testing—"

"Mara died, and her sister took her place?" Patterson looked at Quinn for confirmation.

He rather enjoyed dealing with people who didn't need things spelled out for them, Quinn thought. Such a rarity. "Yes."

"Why?" Patterson asked.

"Because whoever killed Mara was gunning for Mallory," Hannah answered for Quinn, her sharp mind racing ahead, as usual.

"And still is?" Patterson guessed.

"If you know how to reach your brother-in-law, do it. Contact him and let him know what he's up against. Because I can promise you, Mallory Jennings trusts no one. She's not likely to tell him the truth."

"Which means he may not even know what kind of danger he's in." Hannah finished the thought for him.

"Can you reach him?" Quinn asked, looking pointedly at the cell phone lying on the table between the two beds.

"Thank you for the information, Mr. Quinn."

Patterson rose from the bed and gave a dismissive nod. "Good night."

Tamping down a burst of annoyance that burned like fire in his chest, Quinn rose and let Patterson see him to the door. He didn't need to be here in the room to monitor phone communications between Patterson's phone and his brother-in-law's.

He hadn't been a spy for years for nothing.

Nicholas Darcy waited for him behind the wheel of a sleek black Mercedes-Benz car. Quinn slid into the passenger seat and looked at the former Diplomatic Security Service agent, who was the only of his agents besides Anson Daughtry who knew the truth about Mallory Jennings. "Any luck?"

"They're smart people. They understand the risk to Drummond."

Darcy glanced at the recording equipment set up in the backseat of the sedan and tapped the earpiece in his right ear. "Right now they're discussing the wisdom of trying to contact Jack."

Quinn finally let himself smile. "They don't trust me."

"Who does?" Darcy shot him a wry look.

"Fair enough." He pulled out a set of earplugs and plugged them into the recorder to hear what the listening device he'd planted under the hotel room chair was picking up.

In the hotel room, Hannah and Riley Patterson had gone momentarily silent. The light in their room window went dark. Over the strong signal from the bug, Quinn heard the creak of bedsprings and the rustle of fabric, then Hannah Patterson's soft, sleepy query. "Do you want to try another part of the lake tomorrow? Someone at the bait shop said the crappie have really been biting in the flats on the southern end of the lake."

"Sounds like a plan." There was the soft, unmistakable sound of a kiss; then the room settled into silence again. Then, softly, Hannah Patterson murmured, "Good night, Quinn."

Darcy began to laugh softly.

A SOFT HUM roused Jack from a light doze. He felt a vibration against his chest and pulled his phone from the chest pocket of his T-shirt. There was a text message from an unfamiliar name. The message itself was short and to the point. R and I must go radio silent awhile. Take care. She's not who you think.

Hannah, he thought. Probably using some sort of unlisted cell phone—she had cousins in the security business, and even her own side of the family had dealt with more than their share of supersecret skulduggery, if Riley's stories were to be believed.

So. Someone had gotten to her and warned her about Mallory. Had to be the boss, right? The ex-spy Mallory didn't think she could trust.

What kind of game was the man playing? Was he trying to get a bead on their location through Hannah and Riley?

He sent a text back to the number Hannah had used. I know. I'm on it. Then he stuck the phone back in his pocket and lay back against the pillows, gazing up at the darkened ceiling.

Outside, the thunderstorm had finally subsided, the rain decreasing until he heard only the sound of a light drizzle seeping through the thin walls of the motel room.

On the other bed, Mallory had settled into a deep sleep, her breathing slow and even. If she dreamed, she showed no sign of it.

What am I going to do with you, Mallory?

She'd chosen to trust him, for the moment. To allow herself some sleep, to rest up against whatever they were going to face next. But he didn't kid himself that she truly believed he was on her side.

She clearly trusted no one.

Not even herself.

She jerked suddenly in her sleep, then sat up in a rush. She sat rigidly upright for a few seconds, and then her shoulders slumped and she turned to look at him, her expression impossible to discern in the darkness. But he heard a taut quality to her voice that betrayed her agitation. "What time is it?"

He pushed the stem of his watch, making the face glow. "Almost five in the morning. You slept a long time."

"I slept enough." She reached over and turned on the bedside lamp, flooding the middle of the room with light.

Jack squinted against the sudden assault on his dilated pupils. "You can sleep a couple of hours more."

"We need to hit the road before morning traffic picks up." She threw off her covers and reached for her duffel bag on the floor. "I'll take the bathroom first."

He caught her hand as she started past him, and she lifted her gaze slowly to meet his. Arousal flickered in the cobalt depths of her eyes, and he felt an answering fire building low in his belly.

He cleared his throat. "Where are we going?"

Her gaze dropped. "I haven't decided."

But she had, he saw. And he had a feeling he wasn't going to like it.

She attempted a smile. "You'll be the first to know when I do, I promise."

He wasn't sure he believed her.

"WE'RE GOING BACK to Purgatory?"

Mallory kept her eyes directed forward, despite feeling the full impact of his questioning gaze as surely as she might have felt a touch of fingers on her cheek. "I realize it seems crazy, given what we've learned."

"I've come to expect crazy from you," he murmured.

They were still idling in the motel parking lot exit, despite the road being clear in both directions. A right turn would send them north, away from Purgatory. Left would lead back to Deception Lake.

"If that was Endrex I talked to last night, he mentioned Resurrection Point for a reason." She tried to sound more confident than she felt. "Maybe he wants me to meet him there."

"Maybe he wants to kill you there," Jack snapped.

She looked up at him then, took in the glowering expression in his dark eyes and realized he actually gave a damn about whether she lived or died.

It was a disconcerting feeling. Even before Mara's death, she'd been living on the outer edge of society, with only a handful of acquaintances and no real friends. The thought of making a real connection with someone, of letting another person see beyond the tough outer layers of her self-protective shell, was utterly terrifying.

And so very, very tempting.

A tense silence descended, broken only by the sound of Jack's thumbs tapping an agitated rhythm on the truck's steering wheel. She was at his mercy, at least for the moment, and what he decided to do next could change everything.

His eyes drifted closed for a moment. Then he opened them and swung the truck into a left turn onto the highway. "You don't know where we can find a laundry, do you?"

The question, so banal and out of the blue, almost struck her dumb. "A laundry?"

"All I have to live on is a bag of dirty clothes, remember? You'll want me to find a laundry. Trust me on this."

She felt her lips curve, quite against her intentions. She didn't want to smile at him, didn't want to find his dry humor funny. She didn't want to feel anything about him at all, neither anger nor desire.

She didn't want to feel anything, period.

"There's a laundry on the left about a quarter mile up the road. But are you sure it can't wait till we get where we're going?"

"It can wait," he said with a grimace. "But why the hurry now? You really think this Endrex guy is going to be waiting for you on the front porch of your cabin?"

"Of course not," she snapped. "But he may have left a message there."

"Or set up an ambush," Jack reminded her.

"What would you suggest I do? Ignore the message? I need to find this guy. You know why."

"Actually no, I don't." Jack pulled the truck off the road suddenly, parking on the narrow shoulder. He engaged the flashing caution lights and turned to face her. "So why don't we just cut right to it, okay? What do you suspect Endrex may be into here?"

"If we stay parked here on the side of the road, sooner or later a cop's going to come by and start asking a lot of inconvenient questions," she warned.

"So start talking and I'll start driving."

Damn it, she thought. Why was she so tempted to tell him everything she knew? He was such a wild card, a man whose past exploits hardly tagged him as dependable or trustworthy. But there was something about him, a calm doggedness that didn't mesh with anything Mara had ever told her about him, that made her want to spill her guts and hand all her worries to him for safekeeping.

"Endrex was undercover for a while with a

criminal enterprise run by a man named Wayne Cortland." She shot him a pointed look, nodding toward the hazard light switch.

He disengaged the hazard lights and put the truck back in Drive, easing onto the mostly empty highway. "Is that name supposed to mean something to me?"

"Probably not," she admitted. "Cortland's death and the subsequent exposure of his criminal activities was mostly a local story. Out of southern Virginia, really, but Cortland's reach extended to eastern Tennessee and western North Carolina, as well."

"What kind of criminal enterprise?"

"Drug-running, money laundering, general graft. All neatly hidden behind the facade of a successful lumber mill and retail store owned and run by a well-liked and respected businessman. I stumbled onto Cortland's group a couple of years ago while messing around online. There were these anarchists I came across who were passing coded information through a hacker forum I sometimes frequent." She glanced at him to see if his eyes had gone glassy yet. Anyone outside the hacker community tended to tune out after a few seconds, but if he had lost interest, he didn't show it. "I can't say I really suspected they were up to anything bad. Most anarchists aren't really anarchists, you know.

They're just rich kids with way too much time on their hands and no real respect for hard work or civil society."

That earned her a quick sidelong glance. "How bourgeois of you."

She suppressed a smile. "Like I said, I didn't really suspect them of anything. I just like to break codes for fun. I have a database of codes I've cracked over the years—some really easy stuff and some mind-blowing multilayered codes even the government's had trouble deciphering. Anyway, when I was working through this particular code, it occurred to me that I'd seen it before. So I sent through my database, and sure enough, I had. It was one of Endrex's codes."

"And so you decrypted this particular message and—?"

"And it was a plot for a cyberattack on the Oak Ridge National Laboratory. They were planning to use a denial of service attack on the plant's SCADA system—"

"SCADA?"

"Acronym for Supervisory Control and Data Acquisition—it's the computerized system that monitors and controls the plant's critical functions."

"Such as radiation leaks?" Jack guessed, darting another look at her.

"Exactly."

Jack uttered a low, succinct profanity. "I never heard anything about that plot."

"That part never got out to the press. I guess Homeland Security didn't want to start a public panic that might cripple nuclear energy production. Too much was at stake."

"Endrex was part of that plot?"

"That's what I had to find out," she answered. "So I called someone I knew in the government and outlined a hypothetical situation for him."

"Quinn?"

He was quicker-minded than she'd expected. "Yes. Quinn tried to blow it off as the paranoid suspicions of a computer geek with too much time on her hands, but—"

"But you're not the type of computer geek to let a spook like Quinn blow wind up your skirt?"

She couldn't stop the grin at his choice of words. "Exactly."

"And you turned out to be right?"

"I was. And Quinn brought me in on the research."

"What did you find out?"

"That's just it. I wasn't really allowed in on the final findings of the investigation." She released a gusty sigh of frustration. "Apparently in the realm of things I need to know, whether or not Endrex was a black hat wasn't one of them."

"What about now? Quinn's not CIA anymore—and he's still keeping you in the dark? How the hell are you supposed to do your job?"

"My job is to find Endrex, not to figure out his motives." Her tone came out more bitter than she'd intended. Maybe even a little more bitter than she'd realized she felt.

He fell silent for a few minutes, and she took advantage of the lull in conversation to let her eyes drift closed. She was too keyed up to really sleep, but she'd gotten very little rest for the past few days, working late hours trying to track down the elusive hacker. Endrex had always kept late hours, so she'd followed suit, sifting through forums for any sign of his particular style of conversation, with no luck.

Maybe she should have taken Jack's advice and slept a little longer that morning—

"We're getting close to the turnoff to the lake, aren't we?" Jack's tense voice jarred her nerves. She opened her eyes and looked around to regain her bearings, sitting up straight as she caught sight of what had put that note of alarm in Jack's voice.

Ahead, above the tree line, a thin column of black smoke rose into the cloud-strewn sky.

"The turnoff is just ahead." She bent forward, trying to peer through the trees to see what was burning. Hoping she was wrong.

But she wasn't.

Jack slowed the truck, pulling over to the side of the road as they rounded a curve and a Purgatory Fire Department truck came into view, its strobing lights painting the woods with crimson. It was parked on the gravel drive that led to her cabin.

Or, to be accurate, the burning ruins that had once been her cabin.

Chapter Eleven

"Are you sure you can trust them?" Mallory fidgeted on the seat beside him, her restless gaze flicking back and forth between the twisting road ahead of them and the highway they'd left behind.

"Riley and Hannah are the closest thing I have to family." Jack slowed the truck as they approached another curve in the road, missing Wyoming for the first time in a long while. He'd never liked the cold winters, escaping at age eighteen to follow his rodeo dreams in Texas and the Southwest and never really looking back. But the roads there were more or less straight and flat, the vista stretching out for miles ahead, as far as the eye could see.

Here in the Smokies, switchbacks were as common as the never-ending mist that often hid the rounded mountain peaks from view. Narrow shoulders and perilous drop-offs lurked around every bend, setting his nerves on edge as they navigated the road to Purgatory.

"That's not really an answer," she muttered.

"I trust them. They're good people. And they both know a little bit about being under the gun."

He felt her gaze warming him, but the road ahead was too treacherous to spare her a glance. She didn't say anything else for several minutes, but he could swear he heard the cogs meshing in her brain.

"What?" he asked when the silence between them grew oppressive.

"Why were they under the gun?"

They had finally reached a relatively straight stretch of road, giving him the chance to slant a quick look her way. She'd kicked off her shoes and pulled her sock-clad feet onto the seat, her arms wrapped around her knees, keeping them tucked up to her chest. She reminded him of a porcupine he'd spotted once on a hike in the Teton Range, rolled into a defensive ball, all quills and jangling nerves.

He'd avoided injury on that surprise encounter, but he wasn't sure he'd be so lucky this time.

"Which time?" he answered.

She swiveled her head, their gazes clashing for a second before he had to look back at the road. "How many times have they been in trouble?"

"Well, there was the time the serial killer who

killed my sister went after Hannah," he murmured, slanting a quick look her way to gauge her reaction. One auburn eyebrow rose a notch, but she didn't comment. "Then there was the time when a South American drug cartel targeted her family for something one of her brothers did while he was in the Marine Corps."

"You're making this up."

"And there was the time a terrorist took her brother and his wife hostage not far from here to flush out the wife's brother."

She dropped her feet to the floorboard. "Sinclair Solano. Right?"

"You've heard of him?"

"Hard not to—the big showdown took place up in Poe Creek. It was all over the news." Her lips quirked. "Plus, Solano works at The Gates. Just got engaged to another agent."

"Oh."

"He credits his sister's in-laws with saving his hide. So does Quinn."

Jack nodded. "Hannah's one of those in-laws. She and Riley were both here last fall, saving your buddy Solano's ass."

They were nearing Purgatory proper, dense woods giving way to residences, then a handful of businesses that lay on the outskirts of town. Just beyond the tiny downtown lay their next destination, a green park where Hannah and Cody would be waiting for them with Jack's things.

He glanced at her again, taking in her tense-set jaw and stony expression. "What's it going to be, MJ? Stop or keep going?"

She looked at him. "Don't you mean, trust or no trust?"

He nodded.

"Five minutes," she said after a beat of silence. "If you're not back at the truck in five minutes, I won't be here."

He knew she wasn't bluffing.

THE GREEN PARK turned out to be less a traditional park and more a scenic overlook. Jack made his way across the slender ribbon of grass between the small car park and the tree line about thirty yards away. Past the trees was a sharp drop-off plunging toward a shining ribbon of water about thirty feet below the rocky bluff.

"Little Black Creek." Hannah's voice was impossibly close.

He whipped around at the sound and found her standing a couple of feet away, Cody napping against her shoulder.

"What?"

She nodded toward the water below. "It's called Little Black Creek. I read it on a monument plaque back near the parking lot entrance."

Her brow furrowed as she looked him over with sharp eyes, reminding him for a moment of his sister Emily, though Hannah and Emily weren't very much alike at all, at least in appearance. Hannah's eyes were green, not brown, for one thing, and her straight bob of hair was auburn, not dark and glossy as a raven's wing as Emily's had been.

But she had Emily's strong sense of justice. Of the importance of family. Jack liked to think Emily would have been happy to see Riley find love again with someone like Hannah. "You okay?" she asked.

"I'm fine."

"Still want to play it this way?"

"I have to."

"She's not Mara."

"I told you, I know." He leaned a little closer, making a show of tucking Cody's jacket more tightly around his little shoulders. "How did you find out?"

"We got a visit from Alexander Quinn."

Of course. "Did he tell you anything else?"

"Just that she's not what she seems."

No, he thought, *she's not.* "Where are my things?"

"Hidden behind the picnic table about twenty yards behind me." Hannah put her hand on his arm briefly, her touch outwardly light and impersonal. But her moss-colored eyes were dark with concern. "Don't be a stranger. And be careful, okay?"

"You know me. I'm always careful."

She rolled her eyes at him as he turned and walked toward the picnic table she'd indicated. She wandered off, out of sight, and for a second, he felt a gut-twisting fear he would never see her, Riley or their little boy again.

The battered old duffel bag he'd packed for the fishing trip lay under the picnic bench nearest the tree line. Jack sat on the bench a moment, pulling out his phone and making a show of checking his messages, but he was scanning the park around him for any sign of prying eyes.

The park was mostly empty at this time of morning on a weekday, though a minivan pulled up a few parking slots down from where he'd parked his truck. As a harried-looking woman got out of the van and went around to open the side door, Jack caught the handle of his duffel bag and got up unhurriedly.

The woman emerged from around the side of the van with three kids in tow, all preschool aged and as golden-haired as she was. He spared them only a cursory glance as he crossed the narrow strip of grass between the picnic table and his truck.

Sunlight glared off the windshield, making

it impossible for Jack to see clearly inside the truck's cab. He took a quick glance at his watch and saw that six minutes had passed since he left Mallory alone in the truck.

Had she made good on her threat to leave?

The truck looked empty until he reached the door and checked inside the cab. Huddled in a little knot on the floor of the truck, Mallory lifted her head just enough for her blue eyes to meet his.

He released a pent-up breath and opened the driver's door, tossing the duffel bag on the bench seat at the back of the extended cab. "You stuck around. Even though I'm a whole minute late."

"I was in a forgiving mood," she murmured as he slid behind the steering wheel. "Any trouble?"

"Not a bit." He started the truck and backed out of the parking spot, checking for traffic before he eased back onto the main road.

"How do you know there's not a tracking device hidden in there?" she asked a few minutes later. Only then, after they'd cleared the main part of town and headed onto the winding, wooded mountain road leading south to Bitterwood, the next town on the map, did she uncurl herself from the floor and climb back into the passenger seat.

"Who would have put it there?"

She buckled her seat belt. "You said your brother-in-law was a cop, right?"

"A county sheriff's deputy in a little bitty town in Alabama. He's not exactly the FBI." As she opened her mouth to protest, he shot her a quelling look. "And if you tell me to trust no one, I'm going to ask you to hand over your tinfoil hat, as cute as I'm sure it looks on you."

To his surprise, she gave a soft huffing sound of laughter. "Tinfoil would only conduct the mind-control rays, idiot."

He couldn't stop a laugh in response.

"They haven't been in possession of your bag this whole time, have they?" she added in a more serious tone a moment later. "It's been in your hotel room, right?"

"Right. But who's going to put a tracking device in it? I am nobody, believe me. I'm not going to show up on anyone's radar."

"Didn't your brother-in-law say Quinn had been in touch?" she reminded him.

"You think he'd break into my hotel room and put a tracking device in my stuff? Which, I should point out, I left behind when I hared off on the run with you."

"He didn't survive two decades in the CIA without planning for all contingencies." She reached back and grabbed the duffel bag from the bench seat, dragging it forward.

The bag clipped Jack in the side of the head. "Ow."

"Sorry." She didn't sound too bothered about it, he noticed.

"Tell the truth. You really just want to get your hands on my unmentionables," he joked, trying to remember if there was anything potentially embarrassing packed in the duffel. He didn't think so; since the bull-riding accident, his life had more resembled a monk's than a cocksure rodeo cowboy's.

"Yeah, because these really crank my engine," she shot back in an arid tone, waving a pair of blue plaid boxers toward him before she shoved the shorts back into the duffel.

"Not so hasty there, Agent Mulder. Are you sure the government conspiracy hasn't sewn a listening device in the waistband of those shorts?"

"Laugh it up, cowboy." She zipped the bag up again and shoved it back into the space behind their seats. "At the office, Quinn has detection equipment that can sniff out GPS trackers and radio frequencies—pretty much any way you can be tracked electronically, that detector can find it. Which tells me if they can detect that kind of remote surveillance, they're more than capable of remote tracking themselves."

"Why would Quinn want to track you, though? You're working for him, aren't you?"

She sighed, slumping against the back of her seat. "He has his reasons. He's not paranoid just for the hell of it."

He felt a tug in his gut. "You've been following your own agenda, not Quinn's?"

She looked up sharply. "No. I've kept Quinn entirely in the loop until what happened yesterday."

"Then why would he be suspicious of you?"

She tucked her knees up to her body, assuming porcupine position again. He saw a strange vulnerability in the way she held her head, rigidly still but angled slightly downward, as if ready to tuck herself into an even more defensive attitude.

"I wasn't always a white hat," she said finally.

THE SOUTHERN TIP of Deception Lake was little more than a narrow strip of shimmering water that fed into the Caugaloosa River just south of Bitterwood, Tennessee. It seemed to meander haphazardly through the mountains, more like the river it fed than a lake. But the cabin rentals that dotted the southern shore still called themselves "Lakeshore Cabins," Mallory noted as Jack parked in front of the rental office and cut the truck's engine.

"I'll be right back," he said. "Don't lose your train of thought."

Mallory slid lower in the seat until she could barely see over the dashboard, tracking Jack's movements through her narrowed gaze until he disappeared inside the rental office.

She should grab her bags and get the hell out before he came back, she thought. But she couldn't seem to coax her weary limbs to move.

She wondered where Jack was getting the money to pay for a pricey cabin rental. Had bull riding really paid that well? And even if it had, surely after years of hospital bills and not being able to ride anymore, most of his money would be gone by now.

She sat up straight, a new thought occurring to her. As she fumbled with her seat belt, Jack came back out of the rental office and shot her a brief smile as he opened the driver's door.

"We're paid up for three days—"

"How'd you pay for it?"

He frowned at her urgent tone. "Credit card."

She swore, earning a raised eyebrow from Jack. "We've got to get out of here."

"What?"

"Credit cards, Jack. They're just about the easiest thing to track in the world." She tugged her seat belt back into position. "Just get us out of here. Any direction—it doesn't matter."

"Stop it, Mallory." He closed his hand over hers, his grip tight. He turned, catching her chin with his other hand and making her look at him. "You may be on all sorts of radars, sweetheart, but I'm not. I played it your way back at that cheap motel, but this place requires a little more accountability."

"So let's find a place that doesn't."

"We're here already. It's a place to hunker down, get a little sleep and get you set up to do your hacking stuff. Stop seeing trouble everywhere."

If her nerves weren't stretched as tight as a snare drum, she would have smiled a little bit at the awkward tone of Jack's voice when he talked about her "hacking stuff." What she did for a living was as alien to him as riding in a rodeo was to her. They were about as mismatched a pair of conspirators as she could imagine.

But, strangely, the urge to catch his face between her hands and draw him into a hot, deep kiss was almost more than she could resist. She clenched her hands into fists to keep them from following their instincts. "At least tell me you haven't been using that same credit card this whole trip."

"I haven't," he answered, but she could tell he was lying.

"Damn it, Jack."

"Look, it's done." He let go of her face and buckled his seat belt. "Even if someone is tracking my card, surely it'll take a little while for them to actually show up and—do whatever it is you think they're going to do to us. Right?"

She pressed the heels of her palms to her gritty eyes. Maybe she *was* being paranoid. As intrusive as surveillance was these days, even in a free society, not everybody was the target of nefarious forces. Jack was right about one thing—a retired rodeo cowboy wasn't likely to be on anybody's watch list. Only Quinn and two other agents at The Gates even knew her history as a hacker, and as far as she knew, only Quinn knew about her tenuous connection to Jack Drummond. And she certainly needed to catch up on some sleep...

"Mallory, I won't let anything happen to you." Jack's voice dipped to a soft rumble. "You know that, don't you?"

She wished she could believe him. She wished she could relax her own guard for even a minute, let someone else take up the watch.

Jack's had your back. Every step of the way.

She dragged her hands away from her face and turned to look at him. He gazed back at her with warm, dark eyes that invited her in, tempted her to put her life in his hands.

Maybe it would be okay to let go, just for

a little while, a quiet voice in the back of her mind whispered.

"Okay," she said.

Jack brushed the back of his hand against her cheek, the touch light but warm. "Just another quarter mile to the cabin. Then we can rest."

Rest, she echoed silently.

If only she believed it was safe to rest.

THE TWO-STORY mountain cabin was small but well appointed, with a refrigerator, two cozy bedrooms, a large and open main room on the first floor and a luxurious bathroom with a roomy whirlpool tub that put all sorts of highly tempting images in Mallory's brain as she and Jack stood in the bathroom doorway, taking in the decadent sight.

"I might be willing to kill to get first dibs on that tub," she warned.

"I might be willing to share," he murmured.

She slanted a look at him, heat rising up her neck. She couldn't tell if the offer was in jest or serious. She decided to assume the former. "Magnanimous of you."

"That's one word for it." Shooting her a lop-sided smile, he tightened his hold on the bag of groceries they'd picked up—with cash, of course—at the resort's small market. He backed out of the bathroom. "I'll put away the groceries. Save me some hot water."

She'd been joking about killing to take a bath, but now that she was alone with that tub, the temptation was more than she could endure. She closed the door and turned on the water jets, searching the small wicker basket that sat on the sink counter until she found a small bottle of peach-scented bubble bath. She poured a capful into the bathwater, and the smell of sun-warmed ripe peaches rose in a fragrant cloud around her.

She stripped off her clothes and sank into the bath, releasing a sigh of pure pleasure as the hot, scented water embraced her.

Maybe it was going to be okay, she thought as she slipped lower beneath the frothy bubbles. Maybe they really were safe for now.

She should have known better.

JACK HADN'T MEANT to fall asleep, but the second Mallory finished the sandwich she'd made for her dinner, she'd set up her computer on the dining room table, leaving him to fend for himself. When he woke later, the cabin was dark and he could remember maybe a couple of minutes' worth of the basketball game he'd been watching on the cabin's wall-mounted flat screen before he dozed off.

The television was still on, the sound muted.

An infomercial was playing in flickers of bright colors and overly animated acting. Jack pushed himself up to a sitting position on the sofa and checked his watch. Just after midnight. He'd been asleep nearly four hours.

The kitchen was dark, the table now empty. Mallory must have taken herself and her computer to bed.

Jack rose slowly from the sofa, grimacing at the protest of pain in his reconstructed pelvis. The doctors swore the pain would eventually subside to nothing, but Jack suspected they were trying to put a positive face on his slow recovery. He'd talked to a few former bull riders who'd suffered similar career-ending injuries. He knew the pain and weakness might never really go away. But he was still alive. Still able to walk. The injury could have been so much worse.

He grabbed the television remote and hit the power button, waiting a few seconds to let his vision adjust to the total darkness before he started toward the stairs to the second floor.

He had reached the bottom step when he heard a rattling noise behind him. Freezing, he held his breath and listened.

There. The rattling noise came again.

Someone was trying to open the cabin door.

Chapter Twelve

"She's not just being paranoid, is she?" Nick Darcy's deep baritone rumbled in Alexander Quinn's ear as the two men stood side by side at a safe distance from the smoldering ruins of the Resurrection Point cabin, watching the investigators busy at work trying to discover its cause.

"I never believed she was," Quinn replied, though he wasn't telling the whole truth. He had, in fact, thought Mallory Jennings had an overdeveloped fight or flight instinct, from both her troubled childhood and the time she'd spent as a young woman navigating the Wild Wild West of the internet—not to mention a few dangerous places in the offline world, as well. Every connection in the part of cyberworld she'd frequented could be a potential threat. No one was truly a friend in a realm that secretive and fiercely competitive, and over time, she'd made some dangerous enemies.

"Any leads on her whereabouts?"

"She's with the cowboy. That's all we know."

"And you've no leads on the cowboy?" Darcy's faint British accent seemed to wrestle with the word.

Quinn tamped down a smile. "We've got someone monitoring his credit card use."

Darcy arched an eyebrow at Quinn. "Extra-legally, I assume?"

Quinn knew better than to answer a question that incriminating. "They're unlikely to go far from here. Jack Drummond may be restless and looking for adventure, but he's not going to follow her to the ends of the earth out of some misbegotten sense of guilt about her sister's heartbreak."

"Perhaps not. But there might be a motive other than guilt." Darcy turned his back to the ruins to face Quinn. "Mallory Jennings is an attractive woman. And from what I've learned about Drummond since you assigned me to investigate his background, he's not immune to beautiful women."

"He's also not prone to committing himself to any of them."

"People change," Darcy warned.

"I know." *Better than most,* Quinn added silently.

"How serious are you about finding Ms. Jennings?"

Quinn met Darcy's curious gaze. "Very."

"Then why are we here instead of watching the Pattersons' hotel room?"

Quinn smiled. "Who says we're not?"

FOOTSTEPS COMING UP the stairs stopped after the second tread. Freezing in the middle of closing the laptop, Mallory listened.

She heard a faint rattling noise, so soft and distant she couldn't be certain she hadn't imagined it. Easing the laptop onto the mattress beside her, she swung her legs over the side of the bed and put her bare feet on the hardwood floor. She donned her jeans, grabbed the Smith & Wesson pistol on the night table and shoved her feet into her untied sneakers on the way out of the bedroom.

A rush of movement up the stairs caught her flat-footed, and she pressed her back against the wall, lifting the pistol and aiming for the noise.

"God!" Jack's harsh whisper barely registered over the pounding pulse in her ears. In the milky moonlight filtering in from the window down the hall, he was a lean, dark silhouette standing at the top of the stairs with his hands up.

She lowered the pistol. "What's going on?"

"Someone's trying to come in the front door." Jack moved closer, the welcome heat of his body washing over hers. "It could be a guest trying to get into the wrong cabin, but—"

"But we can't take chances," she finished for him. "Don't suppose you have a weapon?"

"In my room." He edged past her and disappeared for a moment into the other bedroom, returning seconds later with a pistol in hand. "Ready?"

"No, but I don't think we have a choice."

Jack led the way down the stairs, his body positioned squarely between her and the door. The rattling of the doorknob had stopped.

On the first floor, they paused at the bottom of the stairs, listening. The only sound she heard was the rush of their quickened respirations.

"Maybe they went away?" she whispered.

"Can't assume that." He reached back and caught her hand, drawing her with him as he edged sideways toward the living area. "Get down behind the sofa, and stay put."

"While you do what?"

"I'm going to check the porch."

She shook her head. "No. Do you want to be shot where you stand?"

"It was probably just a guest who went to the wrong cabin. Realized the key didn't work and moved on."

"Or it's someone with a rifle who doesn't mind shooting you where you stand to get to me."

He flashed her a smile so cocky she felt like punching him. "Think a lot of yourself, don't you?"

"Jack, this is serious."

The smile disappeared. "Believe me, I know that. And you never did tell me what you meant about not always being a white hat. I have to assume, however, it has something to do with what's been going on, because I'm just not buying that a missing hacker and some terrorist plot that may or may not be in the works is reason enough to send a hit man gunning for you."

She feared he might be right. Something about the most recent attacks felt way too personal to be connected to the probing internet searches she'd conducted over the past few months.

God knew, she'd done some stupid, reckless things when she was younger, things that had sent her running to a man like Alexander Quinn for protection long before their most recent association. Things not even Mara had known about.

She'd run afoul of people who put no value on human life at all, people who wouldn't hesitate to kill anyone who got in the way of their goals. And one of their goals, she knew, was making her pay for crossing them.

"Please don't go out there yet," she whispered. "Not yet."

He turned toward her, the darkened room

hiding his expression. But in his voice she heard a gentleness that stung her eyes with unexpected tears. "Tell me what you want me to do and I'll do it."

"We need to go. Now, before it's too late." She started up the stairs at a run, taking them two at a time.

Jack caught her at the top of the stairs, closing his fingers around her arm. "Wait."

She swung to face him, panic swelling in her chest. "There's no time."

"What are we up against?" he asked.

She didn't pretend not to understand what he was asking. "I swear, I'll tell you everything. But right now we have to get moving."

He held on to her arm a moment longer before he dropped his hand away. "Tell me what to do."

"Just pack. Fast as you can. I'll make sure it's clear outside, then I'll meet you at the truck." She pushed past him, her heart pounding with dread.

THE NIGHT WAS clear and cool, a whispery breeze sending a chill up Jack's spine as he hurried down the porch steps and across the gravel drive to where Mallory waited by the truck. She was in motion, moving from foot to foot, her head swiveling as she scanned the woods around them as if she expected an ambush any second.

Hell, maybe she did. Maybe he should be doing so, too.

When he clicked the remote keyless entry device on his key chain to unlock the door, the resulting beep made Mallory jump.

"Sorry," he said quietly, opening the driver's door while she entered the passenger side and stashed her bags on the bench seat. "We have to leave the key to the cabin at the main office—"

"Don't stop," she said sharply, already belting herself in.

"Why not?" he asked as he started the engine.

"Just don't. We'll get the key back to the property managers if we have to mail it, but just trust me. Don't—"

Something hit the side of the truck with a hard thunk. Simultaneously a bark of gunfire rang in the woods.

"Go!" Mallory growled, folding herself forward and dropping her head beneath the window.

He jerked the truck into Drive and hit the gas, spraying gravel behind them as they barreled down the narrow access road. A second crack of gunfire sounded, but he didn't feel any impact on the truck.

"Faster!" Mallory's voice rang with fear, the frantic sound so different from her normal, controlled tone that Jack felt an answering flood of panic rise in his throat. He was going as fast as he dared on the dark, twisting mountain road, but he didn't let up, the trees a blur as they whipped past them on the way to the main highway. "Take a right at the highway!"

When they reached the four-lane, he turned right and slowed to just above the speed limit, earning a growl of protest from Mallory. "What are you doing?"

"Trying to avoid the notice of the Tennessee Highway Patrol," he answered, slanting a quick glance her way. In the glow of the dashboard lights, her blue eyes glittered with fear as she darted quick looks in every direction.

"We're going to have to stop soon," she warned, "so we really need to get as far as we can as fast as we can."

"Didn't you just say no stops?"

She shot him an impatient glare. "Someone was outside the cabin earlier. They could have planted a tracker on your truck. There's a rest stop about ten miles south of here. We can pull over there." She slumped back in her seat and seemed to make a conscious effort to relax, but one knee jiggled restlessly and he had a feeling that if he reached across to touch her, she'd shoot through the roof of the truck.

"Who was that back there in the woods?" He kept his tone even and calm, though his own nerves were so tightly strung he had to consciously will his fingers not to clutch the steering wheel in a death grip.

"I'm not sure," she said after a beat of silence.

"You said you'd tell me everything."

"I will." She turned her head to look at him. "I will. But it's long, it's complicated and I honestly don't know who that was shooting at us back there. Or, for that matter, who went after me yesterday at my cabin."

"Surely you have some idea."

"I have a few."

"A few?"

"I've made enemies."

"Enemies who murdered your sister thinking she was you?"

She was quiet for a long moment. When she spoke again, her voice was raspy and faint. "Yes."

"And you blame yourself."

"Yes." No hesitation, he noted.

A short while later, the rest stop appeared ahead in the truck's headlights. "You sure we've gotten far enough to risk stopping?"

"If there's a tracker on the truck, they'll find us anyway."

"And if there's not?"

"It's worth the risk." She nodded toward the turnoff. "Let's do this, as fast as we can."

Jack pulled the truck into the rest area parking lot and drove around to the back, where the rest area welcome center would hide them from the road.

The surge of pride that swelled in his chest at Mallory's nod of approval was downright embarrassing. But he followed her lead and exited the truck.

She was already searching the truck chassis, running her hand along the bottom of the side panels. "They didn't open any doors, or your alarm system would have detected the motion, right?"

"Right. Or if they'd put any undue pressure on the car, or broken a window or—"

"Doesn't take undue pressure to put a tracker on the underside of the chassis," she noted. "Wouldn't have been that easy to get all the way under the truck on that gravel drive, I suppose. They'd have stirred up the gravel, and I didn't notice any gravel out of place when I looked around while I was waiting for you." She stood up straight and dusted her hands, looking at him over the hood of the truck. "No tracker that I can find."

"You checked to see if the gravel was out of place?" He stared back at her, once again surprised. Though by now, nothing the woman said or did should have come as a shock.

"I thought a tracker might be a possibility. But I didn't get a chance to check before you came outside and then the shooting started." She opened the passenger door and climbed inside.

Back in the truck, he paused with his hand on the ignition key, still thinking about what her last words had inadvertently revealed. Dropping his hand to his side, he turned to look at her, his heart thudding a slow, deep cadence of dread.

Her gaze swept up to meet his, and in her blue eyes, he saw an answering look of apprehension.

"Just how long have you been running, Mallory?" he asked.

She released a quiet sigh. "As long as I can remember."

THE RAIN WAS BACK, peppering the truck's windshield with fat splats of precipitation and blurring the limited view of the world illuminated in the headlights as they neared the Maryville city limits.

"I told you about my mother's death," she said, filling the tense silence that had fallen between them after her last answer. To Jack's credit, he had remained quiet, letting her gather her thoughts, and her courage, before she spoke.

"You did," he agreed.

"We went to live with my aunt and uncle in Amarillo." The house where Mara had lived had belonged first to their uncle, their mother's older brother. He and his wife had been childless, and when he passed away of a heart attack only a month after his wife had succumbed to cancer, he'd left the house to Mallory and her sister.

Mara had lived out the rest of her life there. Mallory, however, had already moved on long before.

"They were very kind to us. They didn't have any children, so they treated us as if we were there own." She tucked her knees up to her chest and wrapped her arms around them. "Mara thrived."

"You didn't?"

"I witnessed my mother's death. Mara didn't." She rubbed her chin against her forearm, trying to shove the image of that night away, tuck it into that dark little cubbyhole in the deepest recesses of her memory where she tried to keep it hidden. "I guess I never really felt like a child after that. I acted out, and my poor aunt and uncle didn't have a clue how to deal with a kid like me. Brain-smart, maybe, but so life-stupid."

"You never got any kind of therapy?"

She managed a bleak approximation of a smile. "A few visits. I proclaimed myself cured and I guess my aunt and uncle wanted to believe it. So they did."

Jack made a little huffing sound but said nothing else.

"I was sixteen when I finished my high school courses. I was a natural student, I guess. Ate up every subject put in front of me and went back for extras. I don't know, I guess maybe I figured if I learned all the secrets of the universe, my life might start to make sense."

"But it didn't."

"No. It didn't," she agreed. "Next, I went to college at MIT."

He released a low whistle. "Impressive."

She slanted a look at him, wondering if he was making fun of her. He looked sincere enough. "Double-majored in computer science and philosophy."

He grinned at that revelation. "Philosophy?"

"I thought it was cool and radical."

"Was it?"

"Not so much," she admitted. "Most of the guys who took philosophy classes did it to score with the girls."

"That's pretty much the reason guys take any college classes," he murmured drily.

"I graduated from college by the age of nineteen. The world was my oyster, or so the astronaut who spoke at graduation told us." She sounded terribly cynical for a woman not yet thirty, she thought, tightening her grip on her knees. "By then, I had fallen in with a group of hackers I'd met over the course of my studies. Some were fellow students. Some were drop-outs. Some were trust-fund babies with money and time on their hands."

"Black hats or white hats?"

"Mostly gray." They'd played pretty fast and loose with cybersecurity laws those days, too young and stupid to think that anything could ever really touch them. "Nothing that would have landed anybody in jail long-term."

"But short-term?"

"A night in the clink now and then." She shrugged. "I managed to skirt the line. Never got picked up myself." Not by the local cops, at least.

Jack seemed to sense the hesitation in her voice. "Never?"

"Not here," she amended. "In the United States, I mean."

One dark eyebrow notched upward as he shot another quick glance her way. "Then where?"

"Medellín, Colombia."

His voice deepened. "Drugs?"

She shook her head, her gut tightening to a knot. "Guns."

He shot her a hard look. "You were running guns?"

"Not me. Well, I guess I was, but—anyway, the guy I was with at the time was an arms dealer."

He directed his gaze forward again, but she saw in the hard set of his jaw that her confession had disturbed him.

"I didn't know," she added quickly, not sure why she felt compelled to defend herself to Jack Drummond when she'd never felt inclined to explain her choices to anyone besides Mara.

Not even Alexander Quinn had heard a single excuse pass her lips. Nor had he asked for one. All he'd cared about was the information she had been willing to provide about Carlos Herrera and his merry band of arms dealers.

"How'd you end up in jail?"

"Carlos had used me to carry guns. I swear, Jack, I didn't know what he was doing."

He frowned in her direction, as if he found her sudden show of earnestness as unexpected as she did herself. "I believe you."

Relief washed over her like a chill, followed by a flutter of guilt at the part she'd left out of the story. "I wasn't entirely innocent, though."

"Did you think you were running drugs instead?"

"God, no." She recoiled at the thought. "I thought they were smuggling bootleg software. Stuff that should be available open source. Or so I thought at the time."

"Not anymore?"

"Not everything has to be free. People put a

lot of time and sweat into their work. I think they deserve compensation for it."

"Of course."

"But life can look very different when you're twenty-two, foolish and living life in the fast lane." She leaned her cheek against her forearm, ignoring the twinge of pain in her back at her cramped position, another reminder that she hadn't been twenty-two and naive in a long, long time.

"How long were you in jail in Medellín?"

"Four days."

He winced. "How bad was it?"

"Could have been a lot worse," she admitted, thinking of some of the horror stories she'd heard from embassy staff in Bogotá about Americans in Colombian prisons. "One of my friends who escaped the raid called the US embassy in Bogotá. Quinn was there."

"And saw a chance to bring down a gunrunning operation?" Jack guessed.

"Something like that."

"Why do I get the feeling that wasn't the last thing you ever did for Alexander Quinn?"

"Because it wasn't."

"Is that when you went from gray hat to white hat?"

She smiled at the hint of amusement in his voice. She'd known he'd appreciate the hat analogy. "More or less. Quinn saved me from what could have been years in prison. And we took down at least one small band of gunrunners supplying FARC—*Fuerzas Armadas Revolucionarias de Colombia*. Leftist guerrilla group. Very violent."

"Lovely."

"I didn't know."

"Maybe you didn't want to know."

"Maybe," she conceded. "I should have asked more questions."

"You shouldn't have been in Colombia running bootleg software, either," he pointed out in a flat voice.

"And you shouldn't have been messing with Mara's head the way you did," she shot back.

He slanted a hard look her way before the tension in his jaw relaxed and he gave a short nod. "Fair enough."

"No, it wasn't." Guilt tugged at her chest. "You didn't really break her heart, Jack. She never let you that far in."

They had reached the outskirts of Maryville while she was spilling the sordid tale of her misbegotten youth. Ahead, the first traffic light in miles shimmered red in the rainy night, and Jack pulled the truck to a stop and turned to look at her.

"What do you mean, she never let me that far in?"

Mallory made herself meet his curious gaze, even though she felt a ripple of guilt for what she was about to say. "Mara had her own demons, Jack. She was sweet, yes. And kind. But she told me, after you'd left, that she'd never really let herself love you. She knew you'd leave, so she didn't bother. At first, I don't think I believed her. God knows, I hated you for her, because you shouldn't have played with her affections. You certainly didn't care whether or not you left her heartbroken in your wake."

Jack blinked slowly. "I did care. Just too late."

"Well, you can stop feeling guilty now. Okay? Mara never loved you." She waved her hand in front of him. "I absolve you officially."

"I thought you weren't in the absolution business."

"I'm not," she admitted, dragging her gaze away from his warm eyes. She nodded at the traffic light, which had turned green.

With a soft exhalation, Jack drove on, into Maryville proper. Mallory hadn't held out much hope for finding an all-night diner, but just off the main drag, she spotted what looked like a small storefront eatery still open despite the late hour. She touched Jack's arm and pointed.

"You hungry?" he asked.

"I can set up a hot spot there. Get back online."

"And look for what?" he asked, his eyes narrowing.

"Not what. Who." She reached behind her for her backpack and the laptop inside. "It's time to see if Endrex wants to come back out to play."

Chapter Thirteen

Watching Mallory on the computer reminded Jack, unexpectedly, of watching a master bull rider at work. Over the course of his years on the rodeo circuit, he'd seen some rides that defied physics. Observing Mallory's virtuoso turn at the keyboard was almost as exhilarating, though on a more cerebral level. With a few rapid key-strokes, she navigated the internet with both skill and intuition that left him in her virtual dust.

They'd gravitated to a corner booth in the all-night diner, sharing the place with a couple of big rig truckers who were trading highway war stories from their perches on stools at the front counter and a pair of middle-aged lovers more interested in each other than the half-eaten plate of cheese fries in front of them.

He and Mallory had ordered two large coffees and a couple of sandwiches—steak and cheese for him, turkey with Swiss for her—before set-tling down on the same side of the booth like the lovers across the diner from them. But unlike the middle-aged woman, Mallory only had eyes for her laptop screen.

"I wrote a program that logs all my internet interactions. It recorded the brief conversation I had with our mystery contact last night," she told him as her fingers danced gracefully over the keys. "I can run those logs through another program I wrote to see if it can sniff out where the message originated, but it could take a while." She made one final keystroke and sat back, reaching for her neglected sandwich.

"Will that help?" he asked. "Knowing where it originated? I mean, is it going to tell you his physical location, so we could actually hunt him down for a face-to-face meeting?"

"Potentially, yes. But even if his geographic location is masked, we might get some clues about how to make contact with him instead of waiting for him to make the next move."

He could definitely see the benefit in being the ones in control. "How long have you been looking for him?"

"Off and on since the last time he disappeared, which was almost two years ago. But in earnest? The past four months."

"What changed four months ago?" he asked, curious.

"A group called the Blue Ridge Infantry tried

to poison the attendees of a law enforcement conference near Barrowville, just down the road from Purgatory."

"I'm not following."

She glanced at him. "I told you about Wayne Cortland and his criminal organization, didn't I?"

"Right, and you said Endrex worked for him, but what do they have to do with this Blue Ridge outfit?"

"Blue Ridge Infantry. Self-styled patriotic militia, but that's a crock." She grimaced. "They play at their little war games, but they really do it for the money. Cortland figured out how to bring together the interests of three pretty disparate groups of people. There are the anarchists, including hacktivists like the guys whose plot I uncovered. There are the pot growers and meth mechanics who run the drug trade here in these mountains. And there's the Blue Ridge Infantry, who sold their soul to Cortland's organization as the muscle."

"That's a pretty complex organization to run."

"From what I've learned about Cortland since his death, he was strong-willed and charismatic," she continued around bites of her sandwich. "People liked him. Listened to what he had to say. He was also very, very ruthless—while he could be generous with those who did his bidding and acted with complete loyalty, he was swift to punish those who strayed. And his punishments were brutal. People feared his wrath. It gave him a great deal of power."

Her next bite of the turkey sandwich left a smear of mustard in the corner of her mouth. Jack couldn't stop himself from reaching out and wiping it away with the pad of his thumb.

The air between them superheated in the span of a heartbeat.

"I'm sorry," he said, pulling his hand away.

Except he wasn't. He wasn't sorry at all, especially when she reached across the space between them and curled her fingers in the front of his shirt, tugging him back to her.

"Where you goin', cowboy?" she asked in a soft Texas twang that sent shivers up and down his spine.

"You know what a bad idea this is, right?" He didn't hear much regret in his own voice, but he thought someone needed to say the words.

"See, that's the thing." Her words were little more than a soft, hot breath against the edge of his jaw. "Bad ideas are my catnip."

He flattened his hand against her spine, tugging her body even closer. "And how's that worked out for you so far?"

"Hope springs eternal." She punctuated the whisper with a fiery kiss that was pure temptation.

For a breathless eternity, everything around them seemed to disappear into a vortex of sweet, hot pleasure, nothing existing beyond the feel of her lips against his, the brush of her tongue demanding entry, the thud of her pulse beneath his thumb when he closed his hand around her neck to pull her even closer.

A faint dinging noise filtered through the haze of desire, and suddenly she pulled away from him, robbing him of her heat and her touch. He opened his eyes and found her gazing at the computer screen. A small blue dialogue box had popped up on the laptop's screen.

There were six words written there: raindrops keep falling on my head.

Jack looked from the screen to Mallory. Her eyes were bright with excitement, her kiss-stung lips curving at the corners.

"What does that mean?" he asked.

Her only answer was to put her fingers to the keyboard and type in a single word: Helsinki.

"Helsinki?" he asked. "What the hell does all that mean?"

She turned those bright eyes on him, and he felt something crack open somewhere in the vicinity of his heart. "It means we found him," she answered, her smile spreading as surely as the heat flooding through him as he looked into her vibrant eyes. "We've found Endrex."

"And that's good?" he asked, not feeling quite as exuberant. After all, they still didn't know what color hat her hacker friend was wearing these days, did they?

"Better than not finding him, right?" But even as she turned back to the computer, her smile began to fade.

"It could be a trap."

The smile disappeared altogether. "I know. But I'm sick of this limbo. I'm sick of having to pick up stakes and run all the time."

"Four years ago, you didn't know anything about Endrex's involvement in this domestic terror attack, did you?" he asked, wondering why the question hadn't dawned on him before. "You told me you stumbled onto the potential Endrex connection two years ago. After you were already here in Tennessee, right?"

She nodded slowly, not looking at him.

"But Mara was murdered four years ago. And you think the killers mistook her for you."

Her head swiveled toward him, her gaze not quite lifting to meet his. "Right."

"Her death had nothing to do with what we're looking into now, did it?"

"I don't know."

"But—"

Those blue eyes snapped up, wide and scared,

to meet his gaze. "I know it wasn't Endrex who killed her. I'm pretty sure it was Carlos."

"The gunrunner?"

She nodded. "Maybe not Carlos himself, but someone connected to him. When I turned witness against him, he swore he'd make me pay. So I went underground for a long time. And then—"

"And then?" he prodded when she fell silent, worrying her lower lip between her teeth.

"And then Mara called me. She said she needed to hear my voice, and I could tell by the sound of hers she was upset."

"That would have been around the time…" He couldn't finish the thought.

She did it for him. "It was right after you left Amarillo."

Guilt twisted his gut. "I thought you said I didn't break her heart."

"You didn't. She broke her own."

He pushed his hand through his hair, not understanding. "What does that even mean?"

A soft ding from the computer drew their attention to the screen before Mallory could speak. A new message had popped up in the dialogue box. You're in danger.

Mallory's slightly profane confirmation was almost enough to coax a smile from Jack's lips. But not quite.

"Helpful fellow, ain't he?" he asked aloud.

"Because we couldn't figure it out all by ourselves once the bullets started flying."

Another message appeared. Campesinos and rednecks—not that different.

"Campesinos?"

"It's a Spanish word for farmers or farm workers—"

"Hablo español, chica," he drawled. "Rode bulls across the Southwest for years. I know what the word means. But what's the message mean?"

"Campesinos were the lifeblood of FARC."

"The Columbian rebels your boyfriend was arming?"

She shot him a hard look. "My ex-boyfriend. Who was just using me and nearly made me the star of some cautionary movie of the week about the perils of committing crimes in foreign countries with really bad prison systems. And yes, that FARC."

"Surely Endrex isn't suggesting FARC has set up camp here in Tennessee." Although it wouldn't be the first time a band of South American terrorists had ended up in the Smoky Mountains, would it? Just a few months ago, Riley and Hannah had been up to their eyeballs in terrorists from the little South American republic of Sanselmo. "Is he?"

"Not FARC." Her sober tone sent a little chill

up his spine. "I think he's talking about Carlos. Or someone he sent."

"They've found you."

The dialogue box disappeared suddenly. Mallory released a soft growl of frustration.

"What does that mean?" Jack asked.

"He's closed the connection."

"Can you get it back?"

A few rapid keystrokes later, she shook her head. "The link is dead now. He's pulled up stakes."

Jack had no idea what that meant in terms of cyberspace, but the real-world equivalent gave him the big picture. "So he throws out a cryptic warning and disappears. Again."

She nodded slowly. "But maybe it's not so cryptic."

"You've got to be kidding me."

"A few years ago, there were signs that some of the redneck Mafia running drugs in these hills were trying to connect up with some gunrunners from South America."

"What kind of signs? And how do you even know this?"

"Quinn told me about it. Apparently some guy undercover for the FBI infiltrated a family of methamphetamine dealers in northeast Alabama and discovered those meth dealers were in contact with some Peruvian gunrunner. And believe me, if they're looking at that sort of expansion in Alabama, they're looking at it here in the Smokies, too."

Jack's brain was on overload. He was tired, he'd slept very little in the past couple of days and he'd eaten about a quarter of his normal daily consumption in the past forty-eight hours. How the hell was he supposed to unravel the Byzantine workings of a hillbilly crime conspiracy when his brain was screaming for three things—food, sleep and sex—and not necessarily in that order?

Well, food he could handle. His steak sandwich was still sitting, only half-eaten, on a plate in front of him. He grabbed it and downed it in a few bites, ignoring Mallory's puzzled look.

"Finish your sandwich," he said after he swallowed the last bite of his own and washed it down with the cooling coffee. "We can't do anything much until your buddy contacts you again, even if you're right about this gunrunning conspiracy. And neither one of us has had much food or sleep in the past two days."

Or sex, his bleary brain added silently.

Still frowning slightly, Mallory reached for her sandwich.

And another dialogue box popped up in the

middle of the computer screen. It was two sets of five-digit numbers.

Jack's head started to pound. "Zip codes?"

"No, just ordinary code," she answered, a smile in her voice.

A second later, a set of six numbers, separated into twos by dashes, appeared just below the first set of numbers. Finally four more numbers, grouped into twos and separated by a colon, appeared on a third line.

"More code?" he asked, closing his eyes and pressing the heel of his hand to his aching forehead.

Her fingers flying on the keyboard were the only answer she gave. He leaned his head against the padded back of the booth, too drained for curiosity to tempt him back into the hunt. A moment later, she murmured, "He wants to meet."

He opened his eyes. "Where?"

She tapped the set of numbers on the screen. "Lilac Point, tomorrow morning at ten."

"That's what those numbers say?"

She nodded.

"How do you know his code?"

"I cracked it a long time ago. It's one of my hobbies, remember. Breaking codes. I told you, I have a whole searchable database full of codes I've broken." Her eyes slanted up to meet his, the look on her face somewhere between defiant and apprehensive.

"You're so cute when you nerd out," he said, smiling.

She grinned at him. "Thank you."

His smile faded. "So, where's this Lilac Point where he wants to meet you tomorrow?"

She darted another quick look at him. "It's on Deception Lake. About three miles north of the cabin I was renting."

"I don't like the sound of that. What if it's a setup?"

"What if it's not? What if Endrex has information that could stop this terrorist attack from happening?"

He didn't have a good answer, but he sure as hell didn't want to encourage her to take any more chances with her life. So he remained silent.

She touched his hand where it lay on the table in front of him, her slim fingers warm against his. "I think we have to risk it, Jack."

He blew out a long breath. "Okay. But we need to find somewhere to stay tonight. We need sleep."

And sex, his body reminded him. He shoved the inconvenient craving to the back of his mind, where it lurked impatiently.

"I saw a motel on the way in that looked seedy enough for our needs."

Needs that include sex.

He rubbed his hand fiercely against his forehead. "Right."

"Maybe we'll be able to get two rooms this time."

He overruled his body's protest. "Good idea."

She finished the last bite of her sandwich, downed the rest of her coffee and grabbed the jacket she'd folded on the seat beside her. As she shrugged it on, he dug in his wallet for a tip. His cash was starting to run low, he saw with unease. There was probably enough for another night or two in a cheap motel, but after that—

"You do know why getting two rooms is a good idea, don't you, Jack?" Mallory leaned close to him, her voice like velvet.

He stared at her, unable to find his voice over the feral desire roaring through his brain.

"It's a good idea," she whispered, "because we need sleep. Not sex."

"Right."

She touched his jaw, letting her hand slide slowly down his neck and over his collarbone before her fingertips traced a deliberate path over his breastbone and down to the waistband of his jeans. She hooked her finger in the waistband, just over the button closure, and gave a light tug. "For tonight anyway."

She was already out the diner door, leaving the bell over the entrance jangling, before he caught his breath again.

THE MARYVILLE ARMS MOTEL was better on the inside than its faded, shabby exterior had suggested, Mallory discovered when she unlocked the room door and carried her bags inside. The room was small but smelled clean and looked even cleaner, the rugs spotless and recently shampooed. The bedspread was crisply ironed and smelled freshly laundered, as did the sheets beneath. There was even a complementary mint on both bed pillows.

What there wasn't, sadly, was a big, strapping, gloriously naked cowboy in her bed.

She sat on the edge of the bed and fell back, bouncing gently a couple of times before the springy mattress went still. Staring up, she saw the ceiling was spotless white, without a single cobweb in any of the room's four corners.

Finally a cheap motel room she wouldn't mind getting naked in, and she was all alone.

"Sleep, MJ. Not sex." She muttered the words aloud to the ceiling.

The ceiling didn't respond. And sleep didn't

seem likely to happen any time soon in her keyed-up state.

Pushing herself up to a sitting position again, she unzipped her backpack and pulled out her laptop. Settling cross-legged on the bed, she turned on the computer and reached into the backpack again, tugging on the hidden compartment where she'd hidden the three flash drives she'd filled with five months' worth of case notes.

She inserted the first flash drive into the USB port and had started to pull up the contents window when a message popped up on her screen.

Don't trust Jack Drummond.

Chapter Fourteen

Morning was still a rosy promise east of the Smoky Mountains when Jack answered the knock on his motel room door and found Mallory standing outside, already dressed in brown jeans and a camouflage jacket over an olive-green sweater. Her feet were clad in sturdy hiking boots and her auburn hair was pulled back from her makeup-free face in a neat, simple ponytail. She had her backpack slung over her shoulders, and her jaw was rigid with gritty determination.

Her gaze dipped to take in the sight of his bare feet, then rose to the shirt hanging open where he'd shrugged it on before answering the door. She pasted on a smile that was just short of convincing. "Rise and shine, cowboy."

Extending his arms to clutch the door frame on either side, Jack sighed. "It's five-thirty, MJ. The point of trying to get some sleep last night was to, you know, get some sleep."

She didn't wait for him to invite her in, ducking under his arm. "I want to get there well ahead of Endrex."

"In case there's an ambush planned?"

"Exactly."

He closed the door, shutting out the faint light of daybreak and plunging the room into darkness. A second later, Mallory turned on the light by his unmade bed and settled on the edge, looking tense but implacable. Her gaze fixed on the wall across from her, as if she didn't want to meet his gaze. A queasy sensation wriggled in the pit of his stomach.

"Did you get any sleep?" he asked. She didn't look as if she had.

"I got enough."

"You were on your computer all night, weren't you?"

Her gaze didn't flicker, but he saw the slightest twitch in the corner of her left eye. "No."

Liar, he thought.

"I need your truck keys to put my duffel in there." She looked up at him then, her expression neutral. But secrets lurked behind those cobalt-blue eyes, shifty enough to make the wriggles in his stomach turn into knots.

"I'll grab it for you before we go," he said, suddenly convinced the last thing he needed to do was hand over a means of transportation to a woman who'd already shown signs of wanting to run. "Why don't you go get your other things while I finish getting dressed?"

"I don't mind putting it out in the car. I could take your stuff, too—"

Now he knew she was up to something. "MJ, why do you want my truck keys so badly?"

"What kind of question is that?" No flinch, no shift in expression. Nothing but that tiny twitch in the corner of her left eye.

"Being paranoid, I guess." But he still didn't hand her the keys. "You still have that Smith & Wesson you pointed at me the first day at your cabin?"

She shot him a look that suggested he'd just asked the stupidest question in the history of time.

"Good." He pulled his own Colt M1911 from his bag and strapped the pancake holster to the waistband of his jeans. "Then we'll both be armed."

Her eyes narrowed as she lifted her gaze to meet his. "You're allowed to conceal carry in Tennessee?"

"Yeah. They honor my Wyoming license. Is that a problem?"

"Of course not." She sounded utterly sincere. But he didn't believe her.

"Mallory, are you afraid of me?"

She looked surprised by the question. A little too surprised. "No. Why would I be?"

"That was my next question."

"I'm not afraid of you." Grabbing her backpack, she rose from the edge of his bed and nodded at his still-unbuttoned shirt. "Finish dressing. I'll go get my duffel bag and wait for you at the truck."

For someone unafraid of him, she was all of a sudden in one hell of a rush to get out of his motel room.

He met her outside and unlocked the truck with the remote, but he pocketed the keys before he headed to the motel office to settle up the bill with his dwindling cash. If they had to spend too much more time running, he was going to have to make contact with Riley or Hannah again.

But was that a risk worth taking? He already knew Alexander Quinn probably had someone watching Riley and Hannah as it was.

He'd half expected he'd return to the parking lot to find his truck gone. A woman smart enough to navigate the hacker world could probably figure out how to hot-wire his truck.

But she and the truck were still there. She had buckled herself into the passenger seat and sat almost primly upright, her hands folded on her lap. He stared at her in dismay as he climbed behind the steering wheel.

Where was his prickly porcupine?

He shut the door and put the key in the ignition. But he didn't start the engine. After a few seconds of silence, she slowly turned her head to look at him. The corner of her eye twitched wildly.

"Something happened last night between the time we got our rooms and this morning when you knocked on my door," he said quietly. "You're trying real hard to convince me everything's okay, but you're just not that good a liar."

Her gaze dropped to her lap. "Who sent you, Jack? Was it Carlos?"

He stared back at her, caught off guard. "You think I'm working for your gunrunning ex-boyfriend? Really?"

"Maybe it's not Carlos. Maybe it's somebody in what's left of the Cortland organization. How did they get to you? Did they see you talking to me at the diner and think you could be bought?" She turned to look at him, stark pain in her tear-rimmed eyes. "How much did they offer? What was my life worth to you?"

He reached across the truck cab and cupped her face in his palm. She flinched, but she didn't pull away. "Your life is priceless, Mallory. I would never do anything to hurt you. Or anyone else. Not anymore. I've hurt enough people for one lifetime."

A tiny crease formed in the skin between her eyebrows. "You have no idea how much I'd like to believe that."

He dropped his hand away. "But you don't."

She looked at her hands again. "I don't know you. Not really. And what I do know about you doesn't exactly make me want to put my life in your hands."

The truth stung a hell of a lot more than he had expected. "What happened last night? At least tell me that much."

She bent down and reached into her backpack. For a heart-stopping second, he was certain she was going to come back with her Smith & Wesson pistol in her hand, but instead she pulled her laptop computer onto her knees. Opening the computer, she ran her finger across the touchpad and woke the screen, then clicked around until she brought up an image.

"I didn't want to leave the dialogue box open," she said quietly, turning the monitor toward him. "But I made a screen grab."

He leaned closer to get a better look. The image showed a message box in the middle of the computer screen with just four words typed within.

Don't trust Jack Drummond.

A chill fluttered up his spine. "You think that's from Endrex?"

"I don't know," she admitted.

"Did you try to track the message back to its origin?" Even as he asked the question, he realized he sounded like an idiot trying to pretend he wasn't.

Mallory's stony expression shifted, the corners of her mouth twitching as if she were trying to suppress a smile. "I tried. No luck."

"Which means what?"

"Whoever sent it is good at what he or she does." She pulled one foot up onto the truck seat. It was only half a porcupine, Jack thought, but he'd take it. At least it was a sign of thawing.

"I don't know who sent that to you, Mallory. I don't know anybody in Tennessee besides you and my in-laws."

Her brow furrowed suddenly, and she tugged her other leg up to the seat, wrapping her arms around her knees. He managed not to smile at the welcome return of the porcupine position, but some of the tension in his muscles relaxed.

"What are you thinking?" he prodded when she didn't say anything else.

"I told Alexander Quinn about you, Jack. Your name, who you were to Mara—"

"Why?"

She turned her head, resting her cheek on her

knees as she looked at him. "Because I was suspicious of you. Showing up like you did out of nowhere, trying to engage me in conversation. You told me you wanted to talk to me somewhere private. I didn't know—"

"If I was trying to get you somewhere private to do something to you?"

She held his gaze. "Yes. Or that maybe it was a coincidence, and you really didn't know I wasn't Mara."

"But if I kept trying to talk to you, I'd figure it out?"

She rubbed her cheek on her knee. "I moved around a lot after Mara's death. City to city, never sticking anywhere for long."

"Until you stumbled on that plot you were telling me about? The one targeting Oak Ridge?"

"Right. This is the longest I've stuck around any one place in a long time. Probably since college." She lifted her head and looked pointedly at the key in the ignition. "Jack, we're losing daylight."

"So we're back on the same team again?" he asked, resting his hand on the key but still not turning it.

She managed the hint of a smile. "I don't think you're working for Carlos. Or the Cortlands."

That wasn't exactly what he'd asked, but he supposed for his prickly porcupine, it was about as strong a statement of trust as he was likely to get. He started the truck and headed for the highway that led back to the mountains.

BY NINE, THEY had parked near the edge of Lilac Point Park, just off the main parking area. Mallory had directed him to drive past the gravel parking area and position the truck between a couple of sprawling mountain laurel bushes just behind. The bushes wouldn't hide the truck completely, but it was better than sticking out like a sore thumb in the middle of the mostly empty parking area.

"This is a park?" Jack murmured, peering at the narrow patch of browning grass between the gravel parking lot and the rock-strewn banks of Deception Lake.

"So they say." Mallory had unbuckled her seat belt and was now packing things into her backpack, borrowing liberally from both her own duffel bag and Jack's.

"Why are you stuffing all that junk in your backpack?" he asked.

She zipped up the backpack and set it on the floorboard beside her. "Because I'm going to have to get out of the truck to meet him, and if things go bad, I don't want to be out there running for myself without some supplies."

"You're paranoid. Anyone ever tell you that?"

"It's not paranoia if someone's really out to get you." She turned sideways on the truck's seat, pulling her knees up to provide a resting place for her folded arms. She propped her chin on her arms, her restless gaze directed past Jack to the main area of the small park that was visible through the driver's-side window.

"How're you going to spot him if he arrives early?" he asked. "You said you don't know what he looks like."

"I told you a friend of mine met Endrex in person once. She described him to me in detail." Her eyes focused on him for a moment. "I think she thought I was interested in hooking up with him or something."

Jack felt a twinge of annoyance. "Were you?"

"I was on my 'men are of the devil' kick then. *So* not interested."

"Did you ever get off that kick?" he muttered.

"I've come to the conclusion not *all* men are of the devil." She shot him a lopsided grin. "And even the ones who are have their uses."

He was beginning to wish he hadn't asked the question, because the thought of her with another man left him feeling queasy. "Are you seeing anyone now?"

"You think I'd have thrown you down on that motel room bed if I were, cowboy?"

"I don't know," he admitted. "Sometimes I

think I know you as well as I know anyone, and other times you're a cipher."

"I'm a simple woman, Jack."

He could tell by the twinkle in her eyes that she knew damn well she was anything but simple. "Have you ever been in love?"

"Have you?" she shot back.

Not until now.

He straightened his spine, shocked by the thought that had just flitted through his head. In love? With Mallory Jennings?

"No," he answered.

"Me, either." There was a wistful note in her voice that caught him by surprise. It seemed to startle her as well, for she tucked her knees more tightly to her chest and looked away.

"I know that kind of love exists," he said quietly, willing her to look at him again, wanting to read the thoughts her cobalt eyes seemed unable to hide. "My brother-in-law, Riley, found it twice in a lifetime."

"Tell him he's greedy. Some people never even find it once." She bumped gazes with him briefly before she looked away again, but it was enough for him to see that the wistful tone in her voice hadn't been his imagination.

"Maybe we haven't found it because we're not open to it."

One eyebrow arched in skepticism. "Thank you, Dr. Phil."

"I could never have loved Mara," he said a moment later, overwhelmed by the need to explain himself to her. He knew a large part of her opinion of him was based on the way he'd treated her sister, and he didn't want to part ways with her, as they'd have to do sooner or later, without trying to make her understand he wasn't that man anymore.

"Why not?"

"It wasn't that she wasn't lovable. She was. Lovable, lovely—she deserved to be loved by a man who would give her everything she needed."

"You weren't that man." It wasn't a question.

"No. I wasn't," he agreed. "And even now that I've sobered up and tried to change who I am, I still don't think we could have made things work."

"You're right. You couldn't have." Sadness marred her pretty face. "Mara didn't believe in love, Jack. She believed in a lot of things I didn't, like hope and patience and all those lovely virtues, but she didn't believe in love. Not after what my father did. She would never have loved you. She picked you because she knew you'd never ask it of her."

Jack stared at her, not certain he believed her. Was she telling him these secrets about Mara to put his mind at ease? To absolve his guilt? "That doesn't sound like Mara."

"You never knew Mara, Jack." She reached across the truck cab and touched his shoulder. "She never let you."

"Why are you telling me this?"

"Because I've spent the past four years hating you. And you're nothing like the man I thought you'd be." She pulled her hand back, closed it around her elbow and rested her chin on his arms again. "I thought you knew about her past. She told me you didn't, but she had a way of telling lies when she was trying to protect people. And I know she was trying to protect you."

He shook his head. "I didn't deserve it."

"I didn't deserve the way she protected me, either."

"I know she loved you."

Mallory shot him a bleak smile. "She had to. I was all the family she had left."

The sadness in her eyes was more than Jack could bear. He reached across the space between them and cupped her cheek again. "She loved you because you're you. And because you're not as unlovable as you seem to think you are."

She blinked a couple of times and pulled away. "As flattering as that sounds, we're not here to have a heart-to-heart."

He dropped his hand to his lap again. "So, what does this Endrex person look like, anyway?"

Mallory's eyes widened as she gazed past him. "Like that," she said with a nod.

He followed her gaze. About fifty yards away, a thin, gangly man in his midthirties walked slowly toward them across the fading grass. He had sandy-blond hair, parted in the middle and pulled back behind his neck, probably in a ponytail, though from the front, it wasn't readily obvious. He was dressed in jeans and a faded green Army jacket over what looked like a graphic T-shirt.

He stopped suddenly, and Jack realized Endrex had spotted the hidden truck. "He's early, too."

"Probably for the same reason," Mallory said. "I have to go to him alone."

"No."

"Jack, if he sees someone he's not expecting, he'll run."

"He's already seen me. I think we have to play it straightforward." Jack opened the door.

Mallory scooted out of her side of the truck and hurried around to meet him, her gaze still locked with the long-haired man who had frozen in place, staring back at them, wide-eyed, like a cornered animal.

Jack held back, letting Mallory move ahead

toward the wary man. She said something to him that Jack couldn't hear, but whatever it was made the sandy-haired man relax a little.

Mallory turned and looked over her shoulder at Jack, giving a slight nod. He picked up his pace until he could see the clear green color of the other man's eyes.

Endrex let his gaze glance across Jack's face before it flicked back toward Mallory. "I need this information to get to the right hands," he said in a soft-spoken, uninflected tenor.

"What are the right hands?" Jack asked.

Endrex's gaze snapped toward Jack again.

"This is Jack," Mallory said. "He's a white hat." She slanted a quick look his way, the corners of her mouth quirking upward. "Literally."

"I was a rodeo cowboy," Jack explained.

"Quaint," was all Endrex said before turning his gaze back to Mallory. "I know Quinn isn't sure he can trust me. I know why, but this is legit, and it's big, and Quinn needs to get his hands on this information as soon as you can get it to him."

"Okay," Mallory said with a nod, but there was an odd note in her voice that Jack had come to recognize as a sign of deception.

She was lying to Endrex. She had no intention of taking whatever Endrex was peddling to Alexander Quinn.

But why?

Endrex reached into the front pocket of his faded jeans and withdrew a small black flash drive. "There are photos on that drive of a man named Albert Morris. He's a US senator here in Tennessee, and he is not the man he claims to be. A friend of mine lost his life getting me those photos."

"Photos of what?" Jack asked.

Endrex kept his eyes on Mallory. "Of Albert Morris and a man named Carlos Herrera."

Mallory's spine stiffened, but she showed no other sign of recognizing the name. "Who's Carlos Herrera?"

Endrex's eyes narrowed. "You've heard the name before."

"It sounds familiar," she conceded. "Why would he be meeting with Albert Morris?"

"Herrera used to be a gunrunner down in South America. But these days, he's gotten into cyberterror. And word is, he's planning to hold a major power company hostage."

"What does cyberterror have to do with Albert Morris?" Jack asked.

Endrex finally lifted his gaze to meet Jack's, his eyes glittering like emeralds. "Albert Morris owns a great deal of stock in a company called Cyber Solutions. If Carlos Herrera successfully takes control of Eastern Tennessee Power's

SCADA and shuts down power for half the state, stock in Cyber Solutions will go through the roof. He'll make millions within a few hours."

Jack stared at the other man, his gut twisting. "You mean this is all about money?"

Both Mallory and Endrex looked at him as if he was an idiot. "It's always about money," Endrex said. He handed the thumb drive to Mallory. "Get this to Quinn. He'll know what to do."

He turned and started walking away, his steps swift and sure.

Mallory looked up at Jack, anticipating his unspoken question. "I don't know if we can take this to Quinn."

"Why not?" he asked as they started walking back toward the truck.

Before she could answer, a loud *crack* split the air, and the tree two feet from where Mallory stood threw off splinters, one of the pieces of wood shrapnel slicing across Jack's hand, stinging.

Next to him, Mallory uttered a single, succinct curse and grabbed his hand. "Run!"

Chapter Fifteen

Mallory couldn't be sure from what direction the gunfire had come, but if they could reach the truck, at least they'd have cover and the possibility of holding off the gunman until someone reported the shots to the police.

But they were still ten yards from the truck when the back tire nearest them exploded into shreds at the next bark of gunfire.

Rifle fire, she amended mentally. Whoever was shooting at them wasn't using a handgun.

Jack's hand tightened around hers and he zigzagged to their left, heading away from the truck toward the thicket of trees near the edge of the lake. "Trust me," he growled when she tried to tug him back toward the truck, which might be useless as transportation but could still give them cover.

What's it gonna be, Mallory? Take your chances by yourself? Or trust the cowboy?

She stopped resisting and ran harder to keep up with Jack.

He was hurting; she could tell by the grimace on his face and the low growl of pain that escaped his throat with each breath. He hadn't shown a lot of signs over the past few days of any lingering injury, but a man didn't give up a career he loved if there was any way he could go back to it.

They needed to find somewhere to stop, to hunker down and regroup until they could figure out what to do next. She needed to get the information on the flash drive to someone who could stop the plot from happening.

But was Quinn that person?

And would they ever get a chance to stop running? Gunfire was coming steadily in their direction every thirty or forty seconds, giving them little chance to slow down and look for a place to hide.

Through the trees ahead, she saw the start of a rocky hiking trail that led up a slope of the mountain that rose behind the eastern edge of the lake. Hiking uphill would be an even harder choice than running along the uneven ground of the lakeshore, but there was nowhere to hide for at least a couple of miles along this stretch of the lake, which served as a waterfowl preserve and was off-limits to developments.

About a quarter mile away, there was nothing but sandy shoreline for a half mile, with only a sparse assortment of trees to offer any cover from further rifle fire. If they kept going, they'd be easy targets.

She felt Jack's pace falter as he spotted the open area spreading out ahead of them. He shot a quick, worried look at her.

She gave his hand a hard tug and started running toward the tree-lined slope. "Up!"

With a groan, he made the turn uphill.

The trail up the mountain was full of twists and turns, well sheltered by hickory, maple and pine trees that grew thick in the lower elevations. The slope was a steady ascent but not so steep that they had to resort to a true climb. And she hadn't heard any more gunfire since they started the run uphill. Maybe the shooter's vantage point was blocked in some way by the mountain terrain.

Which meant they just might have a chance to throw the gunman off their trail. But they'd have to make their move now while the gunman was changing positions.

Peering up the mountain, she scanned the tree line, trying to see through the thicket of evergreens that hid the face of the mountain from easy view. What they needed was somewhere to disappear from sight for a few minutes. A sheltered spot or—

There. Where a rocky knob jutted out from the mountainside, she spotted a dark place that might be the mouth of a cave.

"Come on," she urged Jack, pushing him in the direction of the outcropping.

"They've stopped shooting," Jack said, grimacing as his foot hit a patch of loose rocks and forced him to twist his body to keep from falling. She found herself wincing in sympathy as his face creased with pain.

She touched his arm, sliding her fingers down to brush his hand. "They'll start again. But I think we're out of their visual range for now, so we need to get to that outcropping up there as fast as we can."

He followed her gaze, his eyes narrowing against the late-morning sun. "Is that—?"

"A cave? I think so."

The rifle fire didn't resume during the endless minutes it took to close the distance to the rocky knob. In the shadow of the overhanging stone, the opening of the cave became more readily visible. It wouldn't fool the gunman up close, but maybe in the scope, the cave mouth would look like a simple indentation in the rock.

She hoped so. Because once they went into that cave, they would be trapped with no way out.

Jack's gaze locked with hers. "If we go in there—"

"I know. But I don't think we have a better option."

His lips pressed into a tight line, but he nodded at her backpack. "Did you grab the flashlight from the truck?"

"I had one packed already." She pulled the flashlight from the outside pocket of her backpack and walked toward the cave mouth.

Jack pressed close to her, his heat a comforting presence at her back. They entered together, moving slowly while she swept the narrow beam of light across the cave's rocky interior. It was small and damp, but there were several large chunks of rock that would provide somewhere to sit other than the rough, uneven cave floor.

Hobbling toward the largest rock with an approximately flat surface, Jack settled down with a groan. "If we get out of this mess and I ever get back home to Wyoming, I promise I'm going to give physical therapy another go. Scout's honor."

She nudged him sideways and sat on the rock beside him, dropping her backpack to the cave floor. "You were never a Scout."

"True." He looked down at her backpack.

"Please tell me somewhere in that magical bag of preparedness, you packed a bottle of water."

She unzipped the bag and produced one. "I packed four. But we need to make them last, so don't drink all of it at once."

He swallowed several gulps and handed the bottle back. "Did you know about this cave beforehand?"

"No. I just know the terrain pretty well by now. Lots of caves in this part of the mountains, so I figured our odds were good." She took a couple of swigs. "But if anyone finds this place, we're sitting ducks."

"Great." He grimaced.

"Your injury's really hurting you, huh?"

He turned and pressed his forehead against her temple. "I'll be okay. In a day or two."

She nestled closer as he draped one arm around her shoulder, enjoying the heat of his body in the cool, damp cave. "I don't think we can get any sort of phone reception in this cave, but I can give it a try. Though I'm not quite sure who to call."

"I could call Riley. He'd come, no questions asked." Jack's beard stubble scraped lightly against her skin, shooting sparks through her nervous system. "You think there's really a chance your phone can get a signal with all these rock walls around us?"

"Like I said, I can try." She dipped her hand into the backpack at her feet and pulled out the phone.

No bars.

"No reception." Slumping against Jack's side, she pocketed the phone.

"I could sneak outside—"

She shook her head. "Can't risk it. If the shooter's had time to switch to a better line of sight, he'd spot your movement."

"Do you think it's Carlos?"

God, she hoped not. "I don't know. Carlos obviously knows his way around guns, but he liked handguns better than long guns." She'd seen his handiwork up close and personal in Colombia, shortly before the federal police had descended and swept her up in a raid. She'd been so relieved to get away from Carlos, it had taken several hours to realize she'd merely traded one nightmare for another. "But I'm sure he's not the only one that crooked senate candidate has on the payroll."

"You said Endrex was connected to some criminal organization."

"Quinn said he went undercover with Cortland Enterprises, but I'm not sure Quinn trusted Endrex's motives." She shook her head. "But why hand over the flash drive and tell me to give it to Quinn? If he's telling the truth about what's on it, that's the kind of thing a struggling crime ring would love to get their hands on. Imagine if they could get enough dirt on a US senator to put him in their pockets?"

"Maybe Endrex lied about what's on the flash drive," Jack suggested.

She pulled the flash drive from her pocket and unzipped her backpack. "Just one way to find out."

"STILL NOTHING FROM the in-laws?" Nick Darcy's voice was a bit tinny over the cell-phone speaker, but his British inflections would have given away his identity even if the phone number on the cell-phone display hadn't.

"Not so far. They're out on the lake, like it's just another day of fishing." Quinn lifted his binoculars and took another look, just to reassure himself that Hannah Patterson and her husband hadn't pulled a fast one. She was a Cooper by birth, after all, and the past few years had taught Quinn never to underestimate any member of that trouble-magnet family.

"They know they're being watched."

"Of course."

"And the Jennings woman has decamped entirely?"

"If you're asking have I heard from her, no." Nor had he expected to. As disturbing as the attacks on Mallory Jennings were to him, they would be exponentially worse for the woman herself. She knew he'd been worried about a mole in the agency, and it was becoming painfully clear he was right.

And now he had a pair of suspects.

Nick Darcy and Anson Daughtry were the only people at The Gates who had any idea Mallory Jennings was something more than part of the agency's clerical staff. Which meant it was highly likely that whoever had leaked Mallory's whereabouts was one of those two men.

Men he'd trusted as much as he trusted anyone.

"You don't have any idea where she'd go?" Darcy sounded as if he suspected Quinn was being less than forthcoming. The man was no fool.

"The Pattersons are moving positions on the lake. I have to go," he lied, ending the call. He lifted the binoculars again, this time focusing on the back of Patterson's neck.

What he saw there made him sit up straight.

"Son of a bitch," he growled, spotting the black tribal tattoo peeking out from the collar of the man's gray T-shirt.

Riley Patterson didn't have a tattoo.

He picked up his phone and dialed a number. Through the binoculars, he saw Hannah Patterson reach into the pocket of her jeans and pull out her cell phone.

"Spotted the tat, right?" she asked without preamble. "I told Caleb he should put some makeup on it, but he said it felt too girly."

He flipped through his mental dossier on the troublesome Cooper family and came up with one of the Birmingham cousins. One of the older brothers was named Caleb, wasn't he? "Caleb Cooper, I presume?"

"I'm flattered you know my whole extended family tree, Quinn."

"Where's your husband, Hannah?"

"I have no idea."

"You're not a very good liar."

"But I'm a very good wife." She hung up the phone.

Quinn ended the call with a hard jab of his finger on the phone's display screen. Pain darted through his knuckle, reminding him that violence was almost never a good response to frustration.

Almost.

Mallory Jennings was running. It was what she did best, and he'd come to know her well enough over the past few years to be able to make a few educated guesses about where she'd end up next.

But this time, there was a wild card named

Jack Drummond. And what Quinn knew about the Wyoming cowboy wouldn't fill up one page in a CIA dossier, much less give him a clue where he and Quinn's missing hacker had gone when things went belly-up.

He hit the speed dial for Anson Daughtry's number and waited for an answer. After the third ring, the IT technician answered in a distracted baritone, "Something up, boss?"

"Any luck tracking Jennings?"

"None." Daughtry sounded personally aggrieved. He prided himself on his technical skills and hadn't been happy when Quinn brought in an outside hacker to conduct the hunt for the hacker she knew as Endrex.

His real name was Nolan Cavanaugh, and he'd been instrumental in bringing down a dangerously corrupt cabal in the previous US president's administration. He'd also risked his life to expose the Wayne Cortland crime organization a couple of years earlier.

Quinn wanted to believe the man was still what Mallory Jennings termed a "white hat," but he'd seen and done too many questionable things in his own life to truly trust the actions and motives of another person.

Including Mallory Jennings herself.

"Do you think she's gone rogue?" Daughtry asked, his low voice rumbling like thunder through the cell phone speaker.

"Stop tracking her for now. I'm following other leads," Quinn said instead of answering Daughtry's question. He hung up and started the car, shifting mental gears as he pulled away from the lake and started back toward Purgatory.

It was a fluke, really, that made him glance back toward the lake as he was making the turn onto the highway. A flock of mallards that had been foraging in the fallen pine straw carpeting the lakeshore took to flight in a flutter of wings, drawing Quinn's attention. A second later, he saw the reason for their sudden ascent—a lanky man running at a full gallop through the trees near the shoreline, his sandy ponytail flying out behind him.

Son of a bitch.

Quinn jammed on the brakes and jerked the car into a spin, reversing course to intercept the running man.

He'd finally found Endrex.

THE SECURITY SCAN finished without detecting any malicious software on the flash drive. Mallory glanced at Jack before she clicked the icon for the removable drive. "Here we go."

He didn't miss the fear in her eyes. He put his hand on her back, flattening his palm between her shoulder blades. She leaned into his touch, and he scooted closer to look over her shoulder at the computer screen.

The flash drive contained only seven files, according to the disk listing. All large image files. "Start at the beginning," he suggested softly when she hesitated with her finger over the touch pad.

She clicked the first image. An image program opened and the first photograph popped onto the screen, revealing a surprisingly clear image of two men sitting on a bench under a tree. In the background stood the corner of what looked like an old stone building.

Mallory sucked in a sharp breath.

"Is it Carlos Herrera?" he asked, rubbing his hand lightly over her back.

She nodded. "And the guy with him definitely looks like Albert Morris. At least, he looks like the guy in his campaign commercials."

"Do you recognize the location?"

"A park maybe? Somebody at The Gates would know." She sighed. "If I trusted them enough to take it there."

"If we could get in touch with Riley..." Jack paused, realizing what he was about to say would mean nothing to Mallory. She didn't even trust him, not really. She certainly wouldn't trust anyone he'd never met himself, like Hannah's family.

But Riley spoke of the Coopers with the same respect, trust and affection he spoke of his old friend Joe Garrison, whom Riley had known since they were ranchers' sons in Wyoming.

"If we could get in touch with Riley, what?" Mallory asked, clicking through to the next photo, which showed the same two men standing on a metal-truss footbridge over a small creek.

"Nothing."

She looked up at him. "You were going to say something."

"It was stupid. You don't even trust me, so there's no way you're going to trust my brother-in-law's in-laws."

Her lips quirked. "Probably not."

"It's just—Hannah's family has a lot of experience dealing with the kind of trouble we're in now. And if you don't trust Quinn—"

"You think I'd turn to a bunch of complete strangers for help? Right." She arched one dark eyebrow at him before she turned back to the computer screen. "Let's get through the rest of these photos, see if we can figure out where this meeting took place. My laptop battery won't last forever."

The fourth photo elicited another soft intake of breath from her. "I know where these images were taken," she said, pointing to a tall-gabled clapboard building in the background. "That's the stables and carriage house at Belle Meade."

"Belle Meade?"

"An old plantation in the state capital. People, tour it all the time. Carlos and this Albert Morris guy could have arranged to connect on one of the tours. Pretend to hit it off and nobody would have thought anything about it unless they knew who—or more precisely, what—Carlos is." She flipped back through the photos they'd already seen. "I think that footbridge is there, too, and I'm pretty sure that stone building in the first picture is part of the estate."

"Does that help us get out of here without being shot?" he asked.

She shot him a withering look. "No."

"Then maybe you shouldn't be so quick to dismiss my idea to contact Riley." He softened his words with another light stroke of his hand down her back. "If we can get away from these rock walls, I might be able to get a signal on my phone."

She twisted to look at him, her expression dark with worry. "Jack, if you go out there, whoever's got that rifle will see you. Then he'll shoot you. And I don't know what—" She stopped short, her lips clamping shut in consternation.

He cradled her face between his palms, struck hard by what he saw shining in her eyes. He kept his voice deliberately light, though his heart was suddenly pounding against his rib cage. "You don't know what you'd do with the corpse?"

She punched his arm, but her lips curled at the corners, just a bit. "I don't know how I'd have gotten through these past couple of days without you," she admitted in a half whisper.

"Alone," he answered, just as quietly. "You'd have just done it alone."

To his surprise, tears filled her eyes and trembled on her lower lashes.

"We're both too alone in this world, I think," he added, dipping his head until his mouth brushed against hers.

She threaded her fingers through his hair, tugging him closer, parting her lips as he kissed her again, her tongue sliding across his lower lip.

He kissed her deeply, thoroughly, not hurrying the moment. He couldn't be sure how much longer they could hole up here, how much longer either of them would live if the gunman who'd just chased them up the mountain ever figured out where they were hiding, and he'd be damned if he rushed through any of the time he might have left.

With a soft growl of frustration, Mallory pushed away from him to look at him. "You think your brother-in-law can really help us?"

He nodded. "I do."

"Then let's see if we can find another way out of this cave." She stood and picked up the flashlight he'd laid on a nearby stone. She turned it on and swept the beam across the far wall of the small cave, looking for God only knew what. Suddenly she hurried forward, directing the flashlight beam upward.

Jack stood, grimacing at the hard ache that spread through his hips and down his legs. He'd overdone the running and climbing, he thought, especially since he hadn't been back to physical therapy in weeks. But he pushed forward until he reached Mallory's side, following the flashlight beam where it bounced off the roof of the cave.

"There's an opening up there," Mallory said. "It looks small, but I think I might be able to squeeze through. Even if I can't, it might give me enough of an opening to pick up a cell signal."

The opening was about ten feet overhead, he estimated. Not an insurmountable distance, but getting up there using only the contours of the cave wall wouldn't be easy. If she were to fall, she risked serious injury. "There's got to be another way—"

The crunch of footsteps outside the cave entrance stopped him short. Mallory turned to look at him, her eyes wide in the flashlight beam before she extinguished the light. Her hands closed over his upper arms, tugging him closer.

The footsteps stilled. For a breathless moment, there was no sound except the faint, rapid sounds of their breathing.

Then a low, accented voice called from the cave entrance, *"Ven a mí, querida."*

A low moan escaped Mallory's throat, and she tightened her fingers around Jack's biceps.

"It's Carlos," she whispered.

Chapter Sixteen

Jack had never considered himself a violent man, despite years of making a name for himself in a physically demanding sport. "I'm a lover, not a fighter," had always been his mantra, and that attitude had gotten him out of some tight spots in cowboy bars over the years.

But if losing his sister to a twisted killer had taught him nothing else, it had taught him there were times when a man had to make a stand. Nobody had been there for Emily when she needed help. But he was here now, Mallory was in danger and there was a loaded Colt pistol in a holster behind his back.

He reached for the pistol and bent to whisper in Mallory's ear, "If you can get up there and out that cave opening, do it. I'll hold Carlos off."

Her grip on his arms tightened to a painful level. "He's after me, not you. I'll go to him."

As she tried to slip past him, he wrapped his arms around her. "He's not going to let me live.

You know that. Get up to that opening and see if you can get out of here. Call for help. Type the number seven and hit Send. That's Riley's phone number." He pulled one of her hands away from his arm and gave her the phone. "Hurry. I'll see how long I can hold him off."

There was only a little light seeping into the cave from either opening, just enough to see the fear in her eyes. "What if he's not alone?"

"All the more reason to call for help." He gave her a nudge toward the craggy wall. "Don't fall."

She wrapped one hand around the back of his neck and pulled herself up to give him a hard, swift kiss. "Don't die."

Then she let him go and started climbing.

He glanced toward the cave entrance, reassuring himself that Carlos was still outside, before he watched Mallory scramble up the cave wall, her fingers gripping the smallest of indentations and outcroppings to keep from falling back to the floor.

Near the top, where the narrow opening let in a triangular shaft of daylight, a small ledge jutted about eight inches from the wall. She eased her feet onto that rock ledge and tested its strength. Pebbles skittered down, but the rock held.

She gazed down at him, flashing him the grimace of a smile, then pushed herself up until her torso disappeared through the tight opening. A moment later, she stepped away from the ledge.

Jack's heart gave a hard flip as her legs swung back and forth in the air. Then she hauled herself the rest of the way out.

He tried to catch a glimpse of her through the opening, but movement in his periphery forced his attention back to the cave.

A shadow slanted across the entrance, unmistakably human in shape.

"This is your last chance, *querida.*" Carlos spoke in Spanish, his singsong inflection sending a chill racing down Jack's spine. "Come out, or I will come in."

"She ain't alone," he drawled in response, aiming his Colt pistol toward the entrance. He might get only one chance to make a good shot.

"Ah, the cowboy." Carlos answered in English that time, laughter tinting his voice. "You think I am some witless bull you can conquer with your nerve and will?"

"That's the plan," Jack called back to him, sparing a quick glance at the opening in the cave ceiling. He hoped it was high enough that Carlos wouldn't be able to spot Mallory moving around above.

Please, baby, stay out of sight and make that call.

"Too sad for you, *vaquero*," Carlos called, laughter in his voice. "For I am not alone, either."

As Jack tightened his grip on the pistol, three more shadows joined the first, darkening the floor at the cave mouth.

CARLOS'S TAUNTING WORDS carried up the hillside to Mallory's hiding place behind a clump of wild hydrangea bushes growing near the opening in the roof of the cave. She hunkered there with Jack's phone, trying to figure out the unfamiliar workings and starting to tremble with panic.

Carlos wasn't alone. Jack was. And she was stuck up here, trying to call for help with hands shaking so wildly she could barely keep her grip on the phone.

Dial seven and hit Send, Jack had said. She followed the direction and punched the send button, lifting the phone to her ear.

A man answered on the first ring. "Jack?"

"It's not Jack," she said softly. "But he's in trouble."

For a second, there was no response on the other end of the line, and she thought he'd hung up on her. But as the roar of her pulse in her ears became deafening, the man spoke again. "I'm Riley, Jack's brother-in-law. You're Mallory Jennings, right?"

She forced the confirmation past her tight

throat. "Right. Jack's trapped in a cave north-east of Lilac Point Park on Deception Lake. I was able to get out through an opening in the cave roof—"

"Trapped? By a cave-in?"

"By gunmen," she answered tersely, barely keeping the panic bubbling up in her chest from raising the tone of her voice. "More than one. I don't have a visual. Jack is armed, but he has nowhere to hide. They haven't gone in yet—"

"Who are they?" Riley asked.

"A man named Carlos Herrera, for sure. Not sure who he has with him. We need help. He said your wife's family has some experience, but there's really no time."

"I'm three minutes from there. I can bring at least two reinforcements with me. Maybe that'll even up the fight."

"Hurry!" She had punched up the GPS coordinates of her position before she made the call; she rattled off the numbers quickly. "Got it?"

"We're on the way." He hung up.

She pocketed Jack's phone and edged forward until she could see around the sheltering hydrangea bushes. From this part of the mountainside, she couldn't see anything that might be happening beneath the rocky overhang that had obscured the cave mouth in its shadow. Though she'd heard no gunfire, she couldn't be certain

Carlos hadn't already entered the cave and taken Jack prisoner.

Edging backward, she peered through the narrow breach in the cave's roof. With the sun nearly overhead at this time of day, the brightness contracted her pupils, rendering the cave interior little more than an inky abyss. But after a couple of seconds, she spotted movement below.

Jack, she realized, pressing himself as deeply into the shallow recess as he could go.

Carlos's voice called out, audible in two directions, both distant where the sound rose over the edge of the outcropping and louder, echoing off the rocky cave walls below. "Send her out, *vaquero*, and you will live another day. Play hero, and you will die together."

"You watch too many movies, Carlos!" Jack called back. Mallory saw a glint of sunlight bounce off the barrel of his Colt M1911 as he shifted the pistol's aim. "There's no way I'm getting out of this cave alive if you have any say in the matter. We both know that."

He was right, Mallory realized with despair. He was outnumbered, outgunned and completely trapped. There was no way in hell his brother-in-law could form a posse and ride to the rescue in time.

There was only one way she could make sure Jack didn't die today.

She stood up and walked slowly toward the edge of the outcropping, careful not to make any more noise than absolutely necessary. Within seconds, she could see the flattened area just below the overhang, though the rock formation still hid Carlos and his cohorts from view.

She edged sideways, trying to find a vantage point that would bring them into view.

Her shoe hit a patch of loose gravel and slid out from under her, sending rocks and dirt pouring over the edge of the small bluff.

Gunfire split the air, and she pressed herself flat, rolling to one side to get a bead on whoever was taking potshots at her.

There. Just inside the shadow of the overhang. A man held a rifle pointed upward, bearing down on her.

She had one second. One shot.

She took it.

As the second round from the man's rifle zinged past her and smacked into the trunk of a scrubby pine behind her, she took a breath and squeezed off one round. The Smith & Wesson pistol gave a small kick against her palm, easily absorbed, and the bullet flew true, hitting the rifleman center mass. He fell to the ground, blood blooming like a flower across the lower half of his gray T-shirt.

A howl of pain rose from below, and Mallory fell back against the hillside, feeling utterly sick.

Gunfire rang from below. Two muffled shots answered in quick succession, coming from inside the cave. Mallory forced herself up again, edging to a different position in search of a better vantage point.

She saw Carlos on the move, circling around, close to the trees for cover. He was heading toward the rocky incline just east of her position, a large black pistol gripped in his left hand. He was fast with a handgun. Fast and deadly accurate.

And she was scared and shaking so hard she didn't have a chance in hell of hitting her target a second time.

Keeping her eye on Carlos, she tried to aim the pistol and get a bead on him, but the trembling in her hands was proving to be impossible to quell. Giving up on taking a shot, she scrambled backward toward the hydrangea bushes that had given her cover earlier.

They'd be useless now, she knew, no match for a bullet zinging through their leaves and branches. But they'd keep her from Carlos's view a little longer, give her time to think what to do next.

Give her a chance to make sure those shots she'd heard hadn't hit their mark in the cave below.

To reach the cave opening, she'd have to move

from behind the bushes. Her pragmatic side, the one that had led her to sit outside a house engulfed with fire and cry while her sister's body burned, screamed at her to stay put. Let Jack fight his own battles. Her life was the only one she had a chance to save.

But another side of her, a strong, fierce, protective side she hadn't even realized she possessed, refused to listen. Bracing herself for a flurry of gunfire, she rolled over to the cave opening and peered down into the abyss.

In the handful of seconds it took her eyes to adjust to the darkness below, a couple of things happened. Gunfire erupted from the other side of the bluff. Jack laid down answering fire, the muzzle flashes bright in the gloom of the cave.

And running footsteps approached, heavy and swift.

Mallory rolled away from the cave opening, already swinging her gun in the direction of the footsteps crunching up the hillside toward her.

Carlos skidded to a stop, his pistol aimed toward her in steady hands.

Her own hand trembled, but not nearly as much as it had just moments earlier. Maybe her nerves had settled down, or maybe it was just knowing that if Carlos managed to get past her, Jack would have nowhere to hide at all. Whatever steadied her grip, she was grateful for it.

She might not be getting out of this standoff alive, she knew, but if she took Carlos Herrera with her, then her life would have been worth something after all.

"*Querida*, this is so unnecessary," Carlos called from his halted position twenty yards away.

"You think so?" She concentrated on steadying her voice as well as her grip on the pistol. Her voice came out solid, and only the tiniest of tremors in her fingers revealed her fear.

"You betrayed me. You alone. I have no wish to hurt your friend. Just come to me now. Put down the gun. I will not harm him."

"I don't believe you." She shifted the gun downward, aiming for center mass again, as Quinn himself had taught her during a half dozen late-night training sessions.

"Go for the biggest target," Quinn had told her flatly. "You want to do damage. Center of the torso does it, and it's not that hard to aim for."

He'd drilled her in shooting protocols, over and over, until she could recite them in her sleep. Then he'd taken her to the firing range he'd set up a few miles from the office and coached her through about three boxes of ammunition until he was certain she could handle the Smith & Wesson M&P40 with skill and ease.

She'd give anything to have Alexander Quinn

at her back right about now. He might have se-crets. He might be one hell of a good liar. But he'd never let her down when she needed him.

He and Jack Drummond shared that sur-prising trait in common. And this was her one chance to prove to both men that they hadn't made a mistake in risking their lives for her.

This was her chance to prove she wasn't a selfish coward.

She looked up at Carlos, her nerves suddenly rock-steady. Her hands no longer shook. A calm, confident smile spread across her face, her heart-beat slowing down to a normal, even cadence.

As her panic seeped away, replaced by a brac-ing dose of courage, Carlos's feral grin faltered.

"Put down the gun, Carlos," she called. "Put it down now and I won't shoot you."

His smile returned, but there was no con-fidence in his lean handsome face. His gaze flicked from side to side, as he tried to gauge how easily he could make a quick escape.

And that was when Mallory knew she had the upper hand.

Carlos's hands dropped a few inches, then he jerked the gun up again and fired off three quick rounds.

But Mallory had already started to move, rolling to her left and coming up ready to fire.

She answered his three shots with one well-aimed round.

He froze in place, another shot barking from the gun as his hands slowly dropped. The gun slipped from his grasp and his head finally turned toward her new position, his dark eyes meeting hers.

Blood spread rapidly across the center of his olive-green T-shirt, darkening the fabric like spilled ink staining a piece of writing paper as he fell facedown in the trail and went still.

Gunfire continued over the edge of the bluff. More weapons than before, coming from more than one direction, she realized somewhere in the outer reaches of her mind. She heard shouts in English and Spanish. Cries of anger and pain.

But she couldn't rouse herself from her crouch, couldn't lower her outstretched hands still holding the pistol aimed at Carlos's crumpled body.

Slowly she realized the sound of gunfire had faded away, replaced by a buzz of voices rising from the bottom of the bluff. Someone had won the gunfight, she thought.

She hoped like hell it was the good guys.

"Mallory?" For a moment, she thought she'd imagined Jack's voice, had maybe heard it rising from the cave nearby, saying something that sounded enough like her name to fool her hazy mind.

Then he was suddenly there, crouched beside her, one hand closing over hers to remove the gun from her tight grasp. "Are you okay?" He cupped her face in his palm and made her look away from Carlos's body, his dark eyes searching hers for some sign that she was hearing him.

"I'm okay." Her voice came out strangled.

"You're not okay. You're amazing." He caressed her chin with his thumb, his dark eyes gazing so intently into her own that she thought she could drown in them. "That's what Riley called you. Amazing. Calm, direct, giving him exactly what he needed to find us—"

"I like to be thorough," she said softly.

Jack stared at her for a breathless moment, then started to laugh softly. He pulled her into his arms, wrapping his body around her until she felt utterly protected. "You are one hell of a woman, MJ."

"Mallory," she murmured against his throat.

"What?"

She leaned her head back to look into his eyes. "You can call me Mallory. It's my name. And I'm kind of tired of running from it."

He pressed his lips against her forehead. "As crazy as these past few days have turned out to be, I'm so damn glad I ran into you at that diner in town."

"So am I, cowboy." She wrapped her arms around his neck, fighting back a laugh. "So am I."

"Carlos Herrera and two of his henchmen are dead. The other two are in the hospital. Both stable but not out of the woods yet." Alexander Quinn spoke with his back to the room, his gaze directed out the large window in his office at The Gates. Outside, the afternoon was nearly gone, fading into an indigo twilight, outlining Quinn's profile in soft blue.

Jack sat beside Mallory in one of the two upholstered armchairs positioned in front of Quinn's desk, while Riley, Hannah and Hannah's cousin Caleb occupied chairs one of Quinn's agents had retrieved from the conference room down the hall.

"What about the good guys?" Hannah asked.

Quinn turned at the sound of her voice. He looked tired, Jack thought, but he didn't know the man well enough to judge whether it was his normal look or a result of the past few stressful days. "One of our agents took a bullet to the shoulder. He's in surgery, but the surgeons hope the damage won't be permanent. But that puts us an agent down."

"You looking to hire?" The drawling question came from Hannah's cousin. Caleb Cooper didn't look much like the other Coopers Jack had met back in Chickasaw County, Alabama. Though tall and fit like Hannah's brothers, Caleb's lean, rawboned look reminded Jack more of Riley Patterson. Fair, freckled skin, light green eyes and rust-colored hair set him apart from the other Coopers, as well.

"I'm always looking to hire." Quinn looked amused. "But I'm not sure hiring a Cooper is a good idea. Your family has a penchant for finding trouble wherever you go."

Caleb grinned, unfazed. "But I'm adopted."

That explained it, Jack thought.

Quinn shook his head. "It's an acquired trait. But if you're serious, you can pick up an application at the front desk." He shot the man a stern look. "And you'll have to pass a background check."

Caleb just kept grinning.

"What about Endrex?" Mallory spoke for the first time since they'd convened in Quinn's office for a final debriefing. They'd spent several hours that afternoon recounting their story to Ridge County Sheriff's Department investigators before the agency's legal team descended on the station and extracted them all without too much pushback from the deputies.

Jack was a little surprised that Quinn hadn't invited any other agents to this little powwow in his office. Mallory had mentioned something about a mole in the company, hadn't she? Was Quinn hesitant to speak freely in front of his agents?

And more to the point—was Mallory still in danger?

"Endrex is safe," Quinn said, crossing to stand in front of Mallory. His expression softened, just a hint. "Now we need to make sure you're protected, as well. I think you should go to a safe house."

Mallory shook her head. "No."

"I can't assign someone to you 24/7—"

"I don't need a bodyguard. I just need to get my life back."

"You may not have a life if you don't take precautions—"

"Wyoming," Jack interjected.

Mallory and Quinn both turned their gazes in his direction. "Wyoming?" Quinn asked.

"It's a long way from Tennessee. She's got no family there. No friends that anyone knows about. She can stay with a friend of Riley's." Jack looked at his brother-in-law, who gave a swift nod. "The guy is a small-town chief of police. Solid as a mountain. Has a nice wife who's tough as nails, a really cute kid and another on the way. And they live in the middle of nowhere—she could stay there for weeks and probably nobody would ever know she's there as long as she didn't go into town."

"Wyoming." Mallory gave him a considering look.

"I have family up that way. Haven't seen them in a long, long time."

Her lips curved in a faint smile. "And the snows are mostly over this time of year."

"Okay," Quinn said after a moment's pause. "We can arrange that."

"What about the evidence?" Riley asked.

Quinn's sharp gaze lifted to meet Riley's. "It's safe for now."

"You didn't give it to the cops?" Jack asked.

Everybody in the room looked at him as if he'd lost his mind.

"Or not," he added, feeling like a greenhorn.

"I've contacted someone we've dealt with before," Quinn answered. "A senator who'll make sure the information gets into the right hands."

"Blackledge," Hannah murmured.

Quinn shot her a sharp look. "He won't let it fall through the cracks. He may be a manipulative bastard, but he takes the integrity of the office seriously. He'll make sure Albert Morris goes down, and hopefully what's left of Cortland's crime organization is going to learn the meaning of the term 'congressional investigation.'"

"When do you go see him?"

"He's already on a flight down here. I'll hand over a copy before the night is over." Quinn turned back toward the window, his posture dismissive. "You all need to get some sleep. I suggest you do so."

"What about Mallory?" Jack asked as they all rose to leave. "Her home is gone."

"It was never my home," she murmured.

Quinn didn't turn around. "Mallory is free to go where she wants. With whom she wants. She'll do it anyway, regardless of my opinion." There was no censure in the man's tone, only a soft resignation.

"It's not personal, Quinn."

"Trust is a fragile thing. I know." He gave a nod, still not turning to look at her. "Watch your back, Mallory."

Mallory looked up at Jack, her cobalt eyes brimming with fearlessness. "I don't think that'll be a problem."

Jack held her gaze, bolstered by her show of confidence. She trusted him, he realized. And if he was correctly reading the wicked gleam flitting around behind all that certainty, she wanted him, as well.

Not a bad place to start.

Chapter Seventeen

Outside the ranch house, a light snowfall scattered a dusting of accumulation on the scrub grass in what passed for a front yard on the sprawling prairie. Mallory tugged her jacket more tightly around her, even though the house was warm and cozy inside.

"Cold?"

Jack's voice sent heat flooding through her long before he wrapped his arms around her from behind and rested his cheek against hers.

"No," she answered, leaning back against him. "I'm just not a fan of the cold."

He brushed his lips against her temple. "Then Wyoming's probably not the state for you."

There was a bleak tone to his voice that made her stomach hurt. Turning around in his grasp, she slid her hands over his chest soothingly and met his gaze. "I can adapt, you know. It's not cold here year-round, is it?"

His lips curved. "No, not year-round."

"You do have summer, don't you?" She faked a suspicious glare.

"Yes, we do have summer." He laughed, tugging her closer. "And nobody says we have to stay here forever. We just need to keep you under the radar for a while, until Blackledge and his congressional investigation can mop up Albert Morris's mess."

"And we couldn't do that from the Bahamas?" She stroked his neck, letting her thumbs play lightly along the edge of his jaw. "Just picture it. Under the radar…in a bikini."

His eyes fluttered closed. "You are a wicked, wicked woman."

Rising on her tiptoes, she brushed her mouth across the cleft in his chin. "It's your favorite thing about me."

He kissed her, deeply at first, drinking her passion as if he was dying of thirst. But before they generated enough heat to light up Canyon County, he pulled back, finishing up the kiss with a couple of soft nips of her lips. "If you want to leave Wyoming, we can. Anytime."

She shook her head. "I don't really want to leave. I like the Garrisons. And Jane's so close to her due date. I'd love to see little Emily say hello to the world."

A hint of melancholy darkened Jack's smile. "So would I."

"Joe told me Emily was a really special person. I wish I could have met her." Wrapping her arms around his waist, she rested her cheek against his shoulder, feeling sad for them both. They'd both lost sisters to violence, and not even the happiness they had found with each other could erase those losses. "Life isn't fair, is it?"

He rubbed his chin against the top of her head, mussing her hair. "No. But sometimes it can be really beautiful."

"I heard from Quinn this morning, while you were gone."

He drew back to look at her. "What did he want?"

"He's got a freelance job for me if I want it."

Jack let her go and stepped back, frowning. "He's got a lot of nerve."

"He wasn't the one who got me in the middle of all that trouble, Jack. You know that. And if he and Riley hadn't happened to cross paths at the right time, neither one of us might be alive right now."

"You're going to take the job, aren't you?"

"I want to," she said, taking his hands in hers and drawing him back to her. "He needs my help looking into the backgrounds of a couple of his agents."

Jack's eyes narrowed. "Why?"

"Because other than Quinn, they're the only

ones who knew my real identity. But somehow someone in cyberspace found out where I was and what I was doing."

"And Quinn thinks it could be one of those two?"

"He wants to know if it was. He wants me to do a little digging."

"What if he's right? What if the person who tried to set you up figures out what you're up to?" Jack tugged her closer. "I just found you, Mallory. And I can picture myself with you for the rest of my life. You and me, learning things about each other, learning new things together— I've never wanted anything as much as I want that future with you. I thought that's what you wanted, too."

"I do." She wrapped her arms around him and kissed him hard, trying to communicate with her touch what she'd never find words to tell him, no matter how hard she tried. "You know I do."

"But?"

"But someone came really close to killing both of us." She touched his face. "You could have died out there. And I'd never have had a chance at that future you like to woo me with."

He shot her a lopsided smile. "Woo you with?"

"You're a good wooer." Tugging lightly at the top button of his shirt, she smiled up at him. "Among other things."

"Look at you, distractin' the big, dumb cowboy with your sexy talk." He pressed his forehead against hers. "Okay. You want to catch the son of a bitch who tried to kill us. I guess I approve. Under one condition."

She leaned back to look at him. "Careful, cowboy. Don't start slinging around ultimatums. You know those get me hot under the collar."

"Promises, promises," he murmured in her ear. "All I want is for you to include me in this investigation. I know you've been used to going it alone for a long time now, but—"

"Being used to something and liking it are two different things," she said. "I need you to have my back on this thing. Absolutely."

"Always." He stroked her cheek. "When do you need to give Quinn an answer?"

She made a face. "I sort of already did."

He sighed. "Why am I not surprised?"

"Because you're not really a big, dumb cowboy." She tugged him with her toward the window, turning so that she could lean back in his embrace again. "You're a big, smart, sexy cowboy."

"Careful, sweetheart. You're giving this cowboy some naughty ideas."

She tugged his arms more tightly around her and turned her head to look up at him, smiling as he dipped his head to kiss her. "Believe me, it's entirely intentional."

"So, WHAT EXACTLY does that mean?" Nick Darcy rose from the chair, a scowl darkening his face as he bent over Quinn's desk, his hands flattened on the shiny wood surface.

In the other chair, Anson Daughtry sat very still, ignoring Darcy's agitation in favor of meeting Quinn's gaze without changing his expression.

Most people, observing the two men for the first time, might have expected the opposite re-action from each. Darcy, with his clipped accent and neat grooming, his expensive, well-cut suit and Italian silk tie, came across as the urbane professional, unflappable and focused, but he was the one snapping in anger and using his height and size in an attempt to express his displeasure at Quinn's decision.

Daughtry, on the other hand, remained calm and contained, despite looking for all the world like a hillbilly, dressed in faded jeans, a plaid shirt over a white T-shirt and a blue baseball cap covering his shaggy brown hair. He answered Darcy's question in a Tennessee drawl that wouldn't have been out of place at any backwoods honky-tonk in Ridge County. "What it means, Nick, is that Mr. Quinn here is puttin' us on suspension because somebody in this place has been leakin' our secrets to the bad guys like a rusty old johnboat."

Darcy's sidelong glare held all the haughty annoyance of an aristocrat. Which, thanks to his British mother's impeccable lineage, he came by honestly. "Thank you so much for explaining, Anson. I wouldn't have been clear on Quinn's intentions if not for your enlightening rusty-boat metaphor."

To his credit, Daughtry managed not to roll his eyes. "I get it, boss," he said. "You're not in the trust business."

"No, I'm not," Quinn conceded. "Nor am I in the business of making accusations without evidence. Which is why I'm putting you both on paid leave pending our internal investigation. You'll need to turn in your security passes and any keys you have in your possession. If either of you needs to visit the premises for any reason, you'll be allowed to check in and out as any visitor would."

"And be escorted everywhere by another agent, I presume?" Darcy asked, pushing back from Quinn's desk. He sank back in his chair and crossed his arms in front of him, clearly annoyed.

"I don't want to believe either one of you is

the mole," Quinn said. "And it's possible neither of you is."

"But we're the only ones who knew the truth about Mallory Jennings's identity." Daughtry glanced at Darcy. "And you think one of us tipped off somebody who used that computer hacker she was looking for to lure her into a trap."

Quinn nodded. "I have to eliminate the obvious."

"And we are the obvious," Darcy murmured, looking ill.

"I have to do this, Nick."

Darcy's gaze snapped up at Quinn's use of his first name. But his lips twitched at the corners, the first hint that his anger was starting to fade to a sort of bemused resignation. "You're beginning to frighten me, Quinn. I wasn't aware you even knew my first name."

Quinn rewarded Darcy's mild gibe with a smile, though humor was about the last emotion he was feeling at the moment. "I'll oversee this investigation myself. And I'll get through it as quickly as possible."

"Who's going to know we're in the hot seat?" Daughtry asked, showing the first sign of unease since Quinn had told the two agents they'd been put on administrative leave.

"I can't reveal who I put on the investigation.

You know that," Quinn said with genuine regret. He'd been on the receiving end of internal investigations before. They were humiliating and stressful, and he didn't enjoy inflicting the same pain on Darcy or Daughtry. "They're good agents, they have no agenda except finding the truth and they will be fast and thorough."

"I suppose I'm in no position to demand more," Darcy said, subdued.

"It's up to you what you want to tell your coworkers if they ask where you're going," Quinn leaned forward, twining his fingers as he met their gazes, first Darcy, then his brash young IT director. "The agents involved believe they'll be able to finish the investigation within a couple of months."

"A couple of months?" Darcy pressed his fingertips to his forehead. "God."

"I'm sorry," Quinn said. "Truly."

Daughtry gave a brief nod and unfolded his lanky limbs from the chair, starting to dig in the pockets of his jeans. "Who gets our security passes and keys? You?"

"That will be more discreet," Quinn agreed, taking the security pass and the set of keys Daughtry handed to him.

With a tip of his cap, Daughtry left the office in an unhurried, loose-limbed stride.

"How long have you known me, Quinn?" Darcy asked in a low, tight voice.

Quinn met the other man's baleful gaze. "Since Kaziristan."

"We survived a siege together. We've worked other cases, both for the government and for this agency. I had a real career, once. I could have sailed through the Foreign Service, climbed the ladder the way my father always intended, but I didn't want to be the kind of man who went along to get along. You know that. You hired me because of it."

"I did," Quinn conceded, refusing to give in to the niggle of guilt twisting his gut. He wasn't a man who dealt in emotions like guilt or doubt. Decisions had to be made. Most of the time, he was the one who had to make them. Second guesses were a sign of weakness. "I will make this as quick and as painless as possible."

Darcy just stared back at him, his dark eyes blazing with fury. He rose and walked out of the room in stony silence.

The door to the storage closet behind him opened, and a tall, long-legged blonde emerged carrying a small video monitor in one hand and a set of earphones wrapped around the other. She wore a satisfied smile. "That played out exactly as I expected," she murmured in a warm contralto as she settled in the chair Anson Daughtry had vacated and crossed her long legs. "Appearances can be truly deceiving. It's why so many people end up playing the fool."

Quinn flashed a quick smile at her enthusiasm, enjoying the view without being obvious about it. He was too old and too jaded for a woman of her age and spirit, but he found no harm in looking, nor in enjoying her invigorating energy.

"Do you have a feeling one way or the other?" She shot him a curious look. "Never mind. I don't want to know. Might taint the investigation."

He gave a nod of approval. "You've chosen your team?"

She nodded, setting the monitor and earphones on the desk so that she could reach inside the jacket of her pearl-gray silk blazer. She pulled out a flash drive and set it on the desk blotter in front of him. "These two agents are the best fit for what you have in mind. They're uniquely suited to ferret out any vulnerability either man might have."

Quinn's smile faded. While he never dealt in guilt or doubt, he didn't enjoy this particular part of being the decision-maker in a world gone mad. It was possible, even probable, that neither Darcy nor Daughtry would ever trust him again. He might be losing two damn good agents to this internal investigation, even if neither one was guilty.

But it was a chance he had to take. A bad actor had wormed his way into the heart of The Gates, putting the agency's integrity—and the lives of its clients and agents—at risk.

It was time to find the mole and bring him down for good.

* * * * *

Paula Graves's thrilling miniseries,
THE GATES, *continues next month with*
KILLSHADOW ROAD. Look for it wherever
Harlequin Intrigue books are sold!

LARGER-PRINT BOOKS!

GET 2 FREE LARGER-PRINT NOVELS PLUS
2 FREE GIFTS!

♥ HARLEQUIN®

Romance

From the Heart, For the Heart

LARGER-PRINT BOOKS!
GET 2 FREE LARGER-PRINT NOVELS PLUS
2 FREE GIFTS!

HARLEQUIN®

super romance®

More Story...More Romance

YES! Please send me 2 FREE LARGER-PRINT Harlequin® Superromance® novels and my 2 FREE gifts (gifts are worth about $10). After receiving them, if I don't wish to receive any more books, I can return the shipping statement marked "cancel." If I don't cancel, I will receive 6 brand-new novels every month and be billed just $5.69 per book in the U.S. or $5.99 per book in Canada. That's a savings of at least 16% off the cover price! It's quite a bargain! Shipping and handling is just 50¢ per book in the U.S. or 75¢ per book in Canada.* I understand that accepting the 2 free books and gifts places me under no obligation to buy anything. I can always return a shipment and cancel at any time. Even if I never buy another book, the two free books and gifts are mine to keep forever.

139/339 HDN F46Y

Name _____ (PLEASE PRINT) _____

Address _____ Apt. # _____

City _____ State/Prov. _____ Zip/Postal Code _____

Signature (if under 18, a parent or guardian must sign) _____

Mail to the Harlequin® Reader Service:
IN U.S.A.: P.O. Box 1867, Buffalo, NY 14240-1867
IN CANADA: P.O. Box 609, Fort Erie, Ontario L2A 5X3

**Are you a current subscriber to Harlequin Superromance books
and want to receive the larger-print edition?
Call 1-800-873-8635 today or visit www.ReaderService.com.**

* Terms and prices subject to change without notice. Prices do not include applicable taxes. Sales tax applicable in N.Y. Canadian residents will be charged applicable taxes. Offer not valid in Quebec. This offer is limited to one order per household. Not valid for current subscribers to Harlequin Superromance Larger-Print books. All orders subject to credit approval. Credit or debit balances in a customer's account(s) may be offset by any other outstanding balance owed by or to the customer. Please allow 4 to 6 weeks for delivery. Offer available while quantities last.

Your Privacy—The Harlequin® Reader Service is committed to protecting your privacy. Our Privacy Policy is available online at www.ReaderService.com or upon request from the Harlequin Reader Service.

We make a portion of our mailing list available to reputable third parties that offer products we believe may interest you. If you prefer that we not exchange your name with third parties, or if you wish to clarify or modify your communication preferences, please visit us at www.ReaderService.com/consumerchoice or write to us at Harlequin Reader Service Preference Service, P.O. Box 9062, Buffalo, NY 14269. Include your complete name and address.

HSRLP13R

LARGER-PRINT BOOKS!

HARLEQUIN *Presents*

PASSION GUARANTEED SEDUCTION

GET 2 FREE LARGER-PRINT NOVELS PLUS 2 FREE GIFTS!

YES! Please send me 2 FREE LARGER-PRINT Harlequin Presents® novels and my 2 FREE gifts (gifts are worth about $10). After receiving them, if I don't wish to receive any more books, I can return the shipping statement marked "cancel." If I don't cancel, I will receive 6 brand-new novels every month and be billed just $5.05 per book in the U.S. or $5.49 per book in Canada. That's a saving of at least 16% off the cover price! It's quite a bargain! Shipping and handling is just 50¢ per book in the U.S. and 75¢ per book in Canada.* I understand that accepting the 2 free books and gifts places me under no obligation to buy anything. I can always return a shipment and cancel at any time. Even if I never buy another book, the two free books and gifts are mine to keep forever.

176/376 HDN F43N

Name	(PLEASE PRINT)

Address		Apt. #

City	State/Prov.	Zip/Postal Code

Signature (if under 18, a parent or guardian must sign)

Mail to the Harlequin® Reader Service:
IN U.S.A.: P.O. Box 1867, Buffalo, NY 14240-1867
IN CANADA: P.O. Box 609, Fort Erie, Ontario L2A 5X3

**Are you a subscriber to Harlequin Presents books and want to receive the larger-print edition?
Call 1-800-873-8635 today or visit us at www.ReaderService.com.**

* Terms and prices subject to change without notice. Prices do not include applicable taxes. Sales tax applicable in N.Y. Canadian residents will be charged applicable taxes. Offer not valid in Quebec. This offer is limited to one order per household. Not valid for current subscribers to Harlequin Presents Larger-Print books. All orders subject to credit approval. Credit or debit balances in a customer's account(s) may be offset by any other outstanding balance owed by or to the customer. Please allow 4 to 6 weeks for delivery. Offer available while quantities last.

Your Privacy—The Harlequin® Reader Service is committed to protecting your privacy. Our Privacy Policy is available online at www.ReaderService.com or upon request from the Harlequin Reader Service.

We make a portion of our mailing list available to reputable third parties that offer products we believe may interest you. If you prefer that we not exchange your name with third parties, or if you wish to clarify or modify your communication preferences, please visit us at www.ReaderService.com/consumerschoice or write to us at Harlequin Reader Service Preference Service, P.O. Box 9062, Buffalo, NY 14269. Include your complete name and address.

HPLP13R

ReaderService.com

Manage your account online!

- Review your order history
- Manage your payments
- Update your address

Enjoy all the features!

- Reader excerpts from any series
- Respond to mailings and special monthly offers
- Discover new series available to you
- Browse the Bonus Bucks catalog
- Share your feedback

Visit us at:

ReaderService.com

RS13